DOCTOR·WHO

Wishing Well

DOCTOR · WHO

Wishing
Well

TREVOR BAXENDALE

BOOKS

2 4 6 8 10 9 7 5 3 1

Published in 2007 by BBC Books, an imprint of Ebury Publishing.
Ebury Publishing is a division of the Random House Group Ltd.

© Trevor Baxendale, 2007

Trevor Baxendale has asserted his right to be identified as the author of
this Work in accordance with the Copyright, Design and Patents Act 1988.

Doctor Who is a BBC Wales production for BBC One
Executive Producers: Russell T Davies and Julie Gardner
Series Producer: Phil Collinson

Original series broadcast on BBC Television. Format © BBC 1963.
'Doctor Who', 'TARDIS' and the Doctor Who logo are trademarks of the
British Broadcasting Corporation and are used under licence.

The Random House Group Ltd Reg. No. 954009.
Addresses for companies within the Random House Group can be found
at www.randomhouse.co.uk.

A CIP catalogue record for this book is available from the British Library.

ISBN 978 1 84607 348 9

The Random House Group Limited supports the Forest Stewardship
Council (FSC), the leading international forest certification organisation.
All our titles that are printed on Greenpeace approved FSC certified
paper carry the FSC logo. Our paper procurement policy can be found
at www.rbooks.co.uk/environment

Series Consultant: Justin Richards
Project Editor: Steve Tribe
Cover design by Lee Binding © BBC 2007

Typeset in Albertina and Deviant Strain
Printed and bound in Germany by GGP Media GmbH

For my Three Wishes –
Martine, Luke and Konnie

and for my Dad, Alan Baxendale,
for still enjoying Doctor Who

'At the end of this tunnel is the treasure,' said Nigel Carson.

The two men with him started to laugh.

'What's so funny?' he asked. He shone his torch back at them so that he could see their faces.

Ben Seddon was a wiry young man with mousy hair and steel-rimmed spectacles. There was just a hint of derision in his thin-lipped smile. 'Come on, Nigel! Have you listened to yourself?' He adopted a melodramatic tone: '"At the end of this tunnel is the treasure!" Honestly, I feel like a character in a kid's adventure book.'

'Get real,' Nigel said. 'We're talking two million quid in *gold* here. This is strictly for grown-ups.'

'Well, I've always liked a good secret tunnel,' said Duncan Goode appreciatively. He was taller, bigger, with untidy blond hair. There was an amused glint in his blue eyes and he spoke with a soft Welsh accent. 'Especially one that leads to *buried treasure*.' He said the last two words with gleeful emphasis.

Both Duncan and Ben started to laugh again, and Nigel swore at them. 'You weren't laughing when I showed you the map,' he snarled. 'You weren't laughing when I showed you exactly where the gold was hidden and how we could get it. You weren't laughing when you both realised how much we'll all be worth when we find it!'

'Lottery rollover,' said Ben, sounding a little more serious. 'I understood that bit all right.'

'Sorry, Nigel,' said Duncan. 'We're just a bit, y'know, hyped up. That's all.'

'We don't have much time,' said Nigel. 'Let's just get on with it.'

Nigel pointed his torch back into the darkness ahead, but the beam just disappeared as if swallowed whole by a huge, black mouth. In this section of the tunnel, there was just enough room for a man to stand up straight and hold his arms out at the sides. His fingertips could just brush the walls. It was cold and damp and claustrophobic, but none of that mattered.

They were, after all, going to be rich. The plans showed the exact position of the tunnel's end, and the treasure chamber was just beyond that. They weren't far from it now.

Ben was still smiling. 'What are you going to spend your share on, Dunc?'

Duncan had to stoop slightly to avoid scraping his head on the ceiling. 'I dunno. A nice car, probably. Nothing too fancy, mind. I don't want to blow it all at once.'

'You'll be able to afford a whole fleet of nice cars,' snapped Nigel.

'All right, nice cars, *plural*. Oh, and a new house for my mum, definitely. And if there's anything left after that, a Cardiff Blues season ticket. How about you, Ben?'

Ben licked his lips. 'First off, I'll pay all my debts. I've got a student loan like you wouldn't believe. If there's anything left after that, then I might set myself up in business. Computer services, that kind of thing. And the car I'd buy – the *first* car I'd buy – would be one of those slick Aston Martins, like James Bond has.'

'Sounds good. What about you, Nigel?'

Nigel's voice echoed irritably from the shadows ahead. 'What do you mean?'

'What are you going to spend the loot on?'

'I don't know. Does it matter?'

'You must have some idea!'

'There's more to this than fancy cars and presents for your parents.' Nigel looked disparagingly at them again and sighed. 'I sometimes wonder why I brought you two along. You're like a pair of big kids.'

'Sorry Nigel,' they chorused dutifully.

'Shut up. Here's the end of the tunnel.'

Nigel's torch beam flickered across a wall of soil. He played the light all around the area and above their heads. Thin, stringy roots hung down from the ceiling, full of thick cobwebs and tiny, scuttling spiders.

'Yuck,' said Ben. 'Creepy-crawlies.'

'Ignore them and they'll ignore you,' advised Duncan softly. 'Just don't offer them a share of the loot!'

They chuckled again but Nigel held a hand up for silence. 'Belt up, you two. This is it. We're right on top of a pile of eighteenth-century gold that's going to make us rich beyond belief.'

Duncan moved forward, touching the wall of soil, appraising the job as best he could in the meagre light. 'Just a few metres beyond this point, you reckon?'

'That's right. According to Ben's computer model, the treasure chamber's not much further along the tunnel – ten metres, tops.'

Duncan looked at Ben. 'Fair bit of digging.'

'Worth it, though,' Ben said.

'Well, whatever happens – it'll be a laugh, won't it?'

'I'm in this for more than laughs.' Ben was looking serious now, staring at the tunnel end as if he could see through it to the treasure beyond. The proximity of all that gold had dampened his sense of humour. 'When do we start?'

'As soon as you can,' Nigel replied. 'I've arranged for picks, shovels and a wheelbarrow. There are some heavy-duty lamps as well – you'll need light to work by.'

'And what about you?' asked Duncan. 'What are you going to do while we're digging?'

'Maintain our cover, of course. As far as the people up there are concerned,' Nigel gestured upwards, through the roof of the tunnel, 'we're assessing the area for the tourist board. I've booked us into three rooms at the local pub.'

'Hiding in plain view, eh?'

'Exactly.'

'Well, come on then,' said Ben Seddon. 'What are we waiting for?'

Nigel told them where the equipment was and the two

men set off back up the tunnel to fetch it.

After a while, when he was absolutely certain he was alone, Nigel took a small object wrapped in chamois leather out of his jacket pocket. Carefully, almost lovingly, he unwrapped the little parcel.

Inside was the stone.

He honestly didn't know what else to call it. To him, it was always just *the stone.*

It wasn't very big; about the size of a man's heart. It was smooth and dark, like a large pebble, but unlike any other stone it was warm to the touch. Always.

'How close?' Nigel asked in a whisper. 'How close am I now?'

The stone didn't always respond to direct questions. But if Nigel relaxed, if he emptied his mind of all thoughts except for those the stone needed, he could often sense some kind of reply. He rested the fingers of his right hand on the stone and closed his eyes. After a few moments he could feel the heat spreading through his hand and arm, as if thin tendrils of fire were working their way upwards, slowly and inexorably, towards his brain.

It still frightened him when he did this, when he tried to communicate with this lifeless lump of rock. He could feel his pulse quickening, his breath growing shallow, his skin prickling with sweat. It always felt as if he shouldn't be doing this, as if he was attempting something that was strictly forbidden and incredibly dangerous. But, unfortunately for Nigel Carson, that was exactly the kind of feeling that spurred him on.

Slowly, slowly, the warmth entered his mind and, without warning, suddenly gave way to a piercing coldness, as if a steel blade was being inserted into his brain.

-very close-

Nigel opened his eyes. 'It's here, isn't it?'

-just a little further-

'What will I find? What is it?'

-treasure-

'Yes, I know, but...' Nigel swallowed. 'There has to be more, doesn't there?'

-there is more-

A smile began to spread across Nigel's lips. But it wasn't his smile. It was the smile of the stone.

-much more-

'It won't be long now,' Nigel assured it.

-the rising is near-

Nigel didn't understand half of what the stone said to him, but it didn't seem to matter. Yes, it scared him. Yes, it sometimes felt as though he was going mad and there was nothing he could do to stop it.

But no, he wouldn't have stopped even if he could.

Not even when the stone forced its way deep inside his mind and made him fill the empty tunnel with a dark, desperate scream of pain.

ONE

'I wish every day could be like this,' said Martha Jones.

She was walking through the woods, occasionally feeling the heat of the sun on her skin as it dropped down through the bright green leaves above, listening to the sound of the birds singing from the branches and the soft buzz of insects in the undergrowth. It was a lovely day to be on Earth.

Martha Jones had visited the past and the future and alien worlds in distant galaxies. She loved her life, she loved seeing new times and places, but she never minded when the TARDIS brought her back home, as it sometimes did, to England in the early twenty-first century. And that was because Martha knew that it didn't really matter where – or when – you found yourself; what mattered was who you were with.

The Doctor and Martha had already dropped in on the Italian Renaissance, hopped from world to world across the Vega Opsis system, and then visited the Frozen Castles of the Ice Warriors before finally deciding that the day could best be rounded off by a traditional English cream tea.

'With scones,' the Doctor had announced with his customary enthusiasm. 'We must have scones, with strawberry jam and clotted cream! I know just the place.'

And so he'd sent the TARDIS hurtling through the Time Vortex to materialise in this very spot.

And it was, as Martha had already commented, absolutely perfect. At the moment, she simply couldn't wish for anything better.

'Be careful what you wish for,' the Doctor commented. His hands were stuffed in the trouser pockets of his pinstriped suit as he strolled along.

'Why?'

He shrugged. 'Well, I can't imagine ever wanting every day to be the same.'

Smiling in agreement, Martha took him by the arm and pulled him closer. 'Come on, you, I'm hungry. It's nearly teatime and I need clotted cream.'

They were walking down a slope of woody earth that led to a narrow road. A short wade through some ferns brought them to a crossroads. There was a signpost.

'Creighton Mere one mile that way,' read Martha, pointing down the road, 'Ickley five miles that way.'

'Which d'you think?' the Doctor asked her. 'I quite like the sound of Ickley.'

'Nearer the better as far as I'm concerned. Let's try Creighton Mere.'

'I'd keep away from that one if I were you,' said an old, dry voice from the roadside.

There was a man sitting on a stile, half hidden by the hedgerow. He was wearing filthy old boots and a worn-out parka. He was old, with weathered brown skin and matted hair, and sharp eyes peering out from beneath bushy grey eyebrows.

'I beg your pardon?' Martha said politely.

'Creighton Mere,' the old man said. 'Wouldn't bother with it if I were you.' At least, that's what she thought he said. It was difficult to tell, because the huge, tangled beard which surrounded his mouth muffled half of what he was saying.

'Why not?' asked the Doctor.

The old man pulled a face, his lips shining wetly. 'It's not a very nice place to live.'

'We don't want to live there,' said Martha. 'We're only visiting.'

'Hmph,' said the man.

'Besides, it's too far to Ickley,' Martha added. 'And we're walking.'

'You're not walkers,' the old man noted. 'You're not dressed for walkin', either of you.' He pointed an old stick at their feet. 'You got nice shoes on, an' he's got trainers. So you must have a car somewhere.'

'We don't have a car,' Martha said.

'We have a police box,' the Doctor added.

The man's eyebrows drew together. 'Police box?'

'Yep. Big blue one, parked back there. It's better for the environment than a car.'

The old man's eyes twinkled at this. 'You could have a point there.'

'So what's wrong with Creighton Mere, anyway?'

The lips pursed inside the beard. 'Nothing much, I suppose,' he said slowly. 'To look at.'

The Doctor raised an eyebrow. 'Well, we're probably not going to do much more than look at it, are we, Martha?'

Martha was about to say that a cup of tea and a slice of cake wouldn't go amiss, but then thought that might sound a bit unfair to a vagrant.

'Please yourselves, then,' the old man said. 'Don't say I didn't warn you.'

'Warn us?' Martha repeated. 'About what?'

'About Creighton Mere.'

'You haven't actually warned us about anything specific.'

'Well, there ain't anything specific I can warn you about. It's more of a feelin'.'

'Ah!' the Doctor nodded as if he understood perfectly.

'What I'm feeling at the moment is hungry,' Martha said. She turned to the Doctor. 'Let's carry on.'

'Just take care of yourselves,' the old man said, not unkindly. 'In Creighton Mere.'

'Thanks, anyway,' Martha said. She gave the man a little wave, and he nodded at her as they turned to go.

'What was all that about?' Martha demanded when they were out of earshot.

'Oh, take no notice,' the Doctor said airily. 'He's probably been moved on by the locals or something and he's got a grudge against the village.'

Martha shivered, remembering the man's sharp little eyes. They had seemed to look right through her at the end, almost as if he was committing every detail of her to memory.

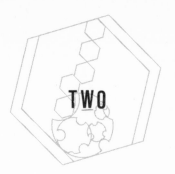

TWO

They had walked another mile or so when a Land-Rover roared around the corner behind them and gave a blast on its horn. The Doctor and Martha jumped out of the way as the battered old vehicle skidded to a halt beside them. In the driver's seat was a beaky-nosed old woman in a bush hat and camouflage jacket.

'Lost?' she demanded through the open side window. The Land-Rover was old and muddy, with wiper-shaped holes in the grime covering the windscreen.

'Er…' said Martha.

'On our way to Creighton Mere,' said the Doctor.

'Well, you're on the right track then,' advised the woman. 'Hop in if you want a lift!'

They climbed in and the woman pulled off before they had properly sat down.

'In a hurry?' Martha asked, wriggling her bottom into the worn canvas of the old passenger seat. The interior of the off-roader was no better than its exterior. Martha guessed the vehicle was genuinely ex-military.

'I'm 83,' announced the woman. 'No time to lose.'

'I like your style,' said the Doctor. He introduced himself and Martha.

'Angela Hook,' the woman responded, swinging the Land-Rover wildly around a sharp bend in the road. She changed gear with precision – Martha noticed that the gear stick was just that; a long, plain metal stick poking out of the muddy footwell – and then floored the accelerator. The vehicle surged forward with a loyal roar and they bounced and bumped over a series of traffic-calming ramps.

'Blasted humps,' growled Angela, jerking in and out of the driver's seat with bone-breaking force.

'I think they're supposed to slow you down,' Martha yelled over all the rattling.

'Rubbish! I preferred it when they called 'em sleeping policemen,' Angela said. 'They just make me want to speed up!'

The Land-Rover rumbled around another bend, and shot through a large brown puddle sending up a spectacular spray of mud.

'We met an old man before,' said Martha. 'A right old scruff…'

'Probably Old Barney,' said Angela without taking her eyes off the road. 'He's been wandering around these parts for years. Harmless but smelly.'

'He tried to put us off coming to Creighton Mere.'

'Did he, indeed? I'll have words with him! Creighton Mere's a lovely place. Miserable old sod.'

'Do you live in Creighton Mere?' enquired the Doctor.

'Born and bred, love, born and bred.'

'Are there any tea rooms there?' Martha asked.

'Not yet,' Angela said, glancing across at her passengers, as if checking them out for the first time. 'But we're working on it. Are you tourists?'

'Sort of.'

'Good! You're just the kind of people we want!'

'Really?'

The Land-Rover emerged from beneath a leafy tunnel into the centre of a small village. Martha glimpsed a large, well-kept rectangular lawn and war memorial, with an old-fashioned red phone box in front of a nice-looking pub, a baker's shop and a convenience store. The steeple of a church was visible above the tops of some trees, and then there was a rather grand-looking house which overlooked everything.

Actually, it was more than a house: behind elegant wrought-iron gates, a gravelled drive led up to the impressive portico of a Georgian manor. Martha got quite a shock when Angela deliberately swerved the Land-Rover past the gates and gave it a series of harsh honks on the horn.

Martha glanced at the Doctor, who gave an amused shrug.

'Sorry about that,' laughed Angela. 'Force of habit! That's Henry Gaskin's place and it's my sworn duty to be as big a nuisance as possible to him whenever I pass by.'

'Ah,' said the Doctor and Martha together, as if this explained everything.

'Don't worry about it,' Angela said. 'Henry Gaskin is a right royal pain in the backside, and he'd do the same to me any day of the week. I'm just returning the favour.'

The Land-Rover skidded to a halt at one corner of the village green and Angela switched off the engine. The vehicle settled with a cough and a rattle and Martha followed the Doctor gingerly out. Her legs were shaking.

'Here we are,' announced Angela briskly. 'Creighton Mere.' She pointed a long bony finger in various directions. 'That was the manor, obviously. There's the pub, opposite the cross. It's called the Drinking Hole, which is a sort of joke.'

The Doctor and Martha exchanged another shrug.

'Those are the shops, for what they're worth,' Angela continued, 'and that's where the Post Office used to be until they closed it down last year due to cutbacks. Damned fools. That Post Office was the nerve centre of the village; it's like cutting out its heart.'

'Oh,' said Martha, her gaze alighting on something nearer to hand. 'What's that?'

'Ah,' said Angela with a little clap of her hands, as if she'd been saving the best for last. 'That's what I'm here for. That's *the well*.'

It looked to Martha exactly as it should – an old village well, albeit in a state of disrepair. It was quite big, about two metres in diameter, with a circular wall around it to about waist height. The brickwork was crumbling in places, and there were patches of lichen and moss clinging to the stones. Two stout wooden pillars stood on opposite sides of the parapet, holding a heavy-looking windlass. There was no rope and certainly no bucket, though. Martha guessed it had been a long time since anyone had drawn water from this well. It looked to have once possessed a little roof of some sort, but no longer.

'It's lovely!' said Martha. 'I don't think I've ever seen a real well before.'

Angela looked admiringly at the well. 'It's our pride and joy – or at least it should be. We're trying to renovate it. As you can see there's quite a lot of work to be done.'

Martha leant on the parapet and peered inside. There was a deep, dark hole protected by a heavy iron grille cemented into the wall at ground level, presumably to stop people falling in.

'Can I make a wish?' she asked.

'You can try,' chuckled Angela. 'No guarantees, mind.'

Martha checked to see what the Doctor thought of it. To her surprise, he was still standing some way back, hands in pockets, staring at the well with what could only be described as a grim expression. 'Hey, Doctor. What's up? Not going to make a wish with me?'

The Doctor didn't reply immediately. His dark eyes continued to stare at the well, and then, with a sudden sniff, he looked up at Martha as if only just registering what she had said. 'What? Oh, no. I don't think so.'

Martha fished in her jeans pocket for some loose change. 'I'm going to,' she said.

'Actually,' said a voice from behind her, 'I'd rather you didn't.'

Martha turned to see a small woman approaching the well at a brisk pace. She was wearing an anorak, old corduroys and heavy walking boots, and carrying a bundle of papers and files under one arm.

'We're trying to check the state of the well-shaft,' the woman added by way of explanation, 'so we don't want all manner of coinage tossed down there, do we?'

'Oh come on, Sadie,' said Angela. 'One more fifty pence piece won't make a difference. Let her!'

Martha smiled. 'Actually, it's a pound coin. Big wish.'

'I don't suppose one more will matter now,' Sadie agreed with a smile, but Martha felt the moment had gone. She'd feel really self-conscious chucking a quid down there now and making a wish. The Doctor watched her with an ironic smile.

'Sadie Brown,' said the woman, offering her hand as Angela introduced them all. 'Actually, this is a genuine wishing well, if you know what I mean. People used to gather round it in times gone by to make their wishes. Sort of a communal thing, I suppose.'

'Did it work?' asked the Doctor. At first Martha thought he was being ironic, but then she realised that he was being perfectly serious.

'Hardly,' replied Sadie with a brief, tight smile. 'In those days the wishes were mainly to do with crops and livestock, with this being a farming area. But farmers are nothing if not pragmatists, and the custom soon died out.'

'Sadie's our expert on wells and restoration and so forth,' explained Angela breezily. 'Together we form the Committee for the Restoration of the Creighton Mere Well. Bit of a mouthful, sorry.'

'There's been a well here since medieval times,' Sadie told

them. 'There must have been natural springs hereabouts, but this particular shaft well has been dry for – oh, well, for as long as anyone can remember. We suspect subsidence or even deep seismic shift is responsible for moving the subterranean springs.'

'It's a pity,' Martha said. 'It looks charming.'

'It'll look even better when we've finished,' Angela assured her. 'Not very many people outside Creighton Mere know about the well, but there are a few people who visit it occasionally. Mostly they're just ramblers passing through. If we can properly restore the well, we think it could be quite a tourist attraction.'

'Well, good luck and all that,' Martha said.

'The Doctor and Martha were looking for tea rooms,' Angela told Sadie.

'Oh, that's not fair,' laughed Sadie, suddenly brightening. 'I'm not ready yet!'

'Sadie runs the bakery here,' explained Angela. 'Her buttermilk scones and toasted tea-cakes are second to none. But she really wants to run a good, old-fashioned tea room!'

'Once I've got the well sorted out,' Sadie added. 'But it's a great idea: The Creighton Mere Well Tea Rooms. Sounds rather good, doesn't it?'

'Great,' said Martha, feeling a bit let down. Her stomach was going to rumble any second.

'In the meantime I'm afraid there's just the Hole,' said Angela.

'The hole?'

'The Drinking Hole.' Sadie pointed across the green.

'The pub.'

'Hence the joke,' Angela said. 'Drinking hole – well.'

'Actually, I'd love a drink,' Martha said, seeing this as a cue to take their leave. She looked to the Doctor for agreement, only to find him still staring at the well, seemingly oblivious to everything else that had been going on. 'Doctor?'

They watched the Doctor as he slowly walked across to the well and, with some caution, rested a hand on the parapet. He continued to stare at the dark opening, as if challenging himself to look inside, and then, quite abruptly, withdrew his hand. Martha was just about to ask him what the matter was when he turned to her with a sudden, huge grin. 'Dandelion and burdock!'

'What?'

'Dandelion and burdock. Who could resist a drink with a name like that? Dandelion and burdock! Anyway, mine's a large one.' He started across the green towards the Drinking Hole. 'Last one there buys the first round. Come on!'

Shaking her head in despair, Martha started after him.

THREE

'You mean there's supposed to be treasure at the bottom of the well?' Martha sounded delighted.

'So they say,' grunted Angela. They were sitting at a small table in the Drinking Hole. Sadie sipped a sweet sherry, Martha had a mineral water and the Doctor had his dandelion and burdock (with a straw). Angela was gripping a pint of Robber's Slake, a local ale named after a highwayman who had supposedly met his fate in Creighton Mere.

'It's probably a load of rubbish,' Sadie said. They had been discussing the myths and legends surrounding the well, and one of these actually concerned the highwayman's stolen loot. 'Every village has its stories around here. If it's not treasure, it's ghosts, or connections to royalty. You know – Queen Elizabeth I slept here, that kind of thing.'

'People always like stories about lost treasure,' Angela mused.

'What do the legends actually say?' the Doctor asked. His eyes were innocently wide, but Martha knew him well enough to know that he was probing. She wondered what was on his mind. He hadn't looked very happy at the well.

Angela shrugged. 'Usual stuff. Some say it's stolen jewels, others say it's a fortune in gold, all allegedly taken by a highwayman in the eighteenth century. On the run from the authorities, he passed through Creighton Mere and dumped the treasure down the well. When the militia caught up with him he was empty-handed.'

'And they were so cross they threw the highwayman down the well too,' added Sadie.

Martha smiled, but she noticed that the Doctor said nothing. He was staring into the middle distance again, slowly sucking up his fizzy pop through the straw.

'I think the treasure was dug up long ago,' Angela said. 'That's how the Gaskins got so rich.'

'The owners of the big manor?' Martha recalled Angela blasting the Land-Rover's horn outside the Georgian house on the way into the village.

'That's right. Jumped up nouveaux riches. The Gaskins have probably been living off it for two hundred years. They'd deny it, of course. Especially the current incumbent – Henry Gaskin.' She said the name as if it tasted sour in her mouth.

Nigel Carson led the way to the pub. Ben Seddon and Duncan Goode had showered and changed, thankfully, and were probably looking forward to a well-earned pint. Away from the dirt and claustrophobia of the tunnel, the excitement of the project was beginning to come back: they were laughing and joking again, still treating the whole business as some kind of lark, which Nigel found very irritating.

The early evening air was cool, and the sun was just about to go into hiding behind the church steeple as they walked across the village green towards the Drinking Hole. A long finger of light pointed across the grass towards the old well.

Nigel looked at the well as the sunlight made it glow. For a moment, he thought he saw someone standing in the shadows on the far side, watching him from behind one of the heavy wooden pillars. It was an old man with long, tangled grey hair and a beard. He watched the three of them with dark, hateful eyes and Nigel stopped. 'It's Old Barney, isn't it?'

'Get out of here, yer rotten lot,' said the old man.

'Charming!'

Old Barney took an uncertain step towards them. 'You're not wanted here, you lot. Clear off, go on!'

'You're shaking, Barney,' said Nigel. 'Been drinking?

'Never you mind!' Barney raised a trembling fist and shook it. 'Just clear off, you greedy swines.'

'Ah.' Nigel smirked. 'You think we're after the treasure, do you?' When he said the word 'treasure', he raised his hands and made little apostrophe gestures in the air.

Barney's eyes narrowed. 'I don't know what yer want here, but yer not welcome!'

Nigel glanced around him to check that he was alone with the old man and could not be overheard. Then, very quietly, he said, 'Let me tell you a secret, you stinking old fool: there is treasure here, all right. But it's not what you think it is. So don't bother yourself about it, because there's nothing here that's going to be any use to a gin-soaked old fool like you. Got that?'

'You lot don't belong here,' Barney croaked fearfully.

Nigel feigned a hurt expression. 'Don't belong here? But, Barney, neither do you. You're homeless, aren't you? A traveller! As for myself… well, I have a room here at the local hostelry.' He pointed at the Drinking Hole. 'Which is where I'm going now. So – fancy another drink? Just a quick one? First round's on you!'

Nigel laughed at his own joke and then walked away, shaking his head. Ben and Duncan were already waiting for him by the pub.

Old Barney was staring after Nigel with a look of disgust mixed with deep concern.

'What did he want?' asked Ben.

'Nothing.'

Duncan said, 'Poor bloke. Looks like he could do with finding some treasure himself.'

'He's just some stupid old fool,' snapped Nigel. 'Ignore him.'

Old Barney was still glaring at Nigel. Slowly the old man dropped his gaze and turned away.

'Come on,' Nigel said to the others. 'Looks like I'm paying after all.'

There was a buzz of happy conversation in the pub and Martha was enjoying herself. There were no cream teas, but the bar did a nice line in sandwiches, so at least they'd been able to have a bite to eat. The only problem was the Doctor. He seemed unusually quiet, ruminating on something Martha couldn't even guess at. Part of her wanted to ask him about it, but another part of her didn't want to break up the happy atmosphere she was enjoying so much.

'So, Martha,' said Angela. 'What would your wish be? If the well actually worked.'

Martha shrugged. 'Oh, I don't know, really...'

'Come on, don't be shy. Out with it.'

'I can't say. It might not come true if I told you.' Martha's gaze settled on the Doctor's profile once again, and Angela nodded wisely to herself. Noticing, Martha laughed shyly and sat up straighter. 'OK. What would yours be?'

Angela shook her head. 'Oh, you don't want to hear about the wishes of a dried-up old prune like me, dear. The only wishes that count are the wishes of the young.'

'Speak for yourself,' retorted Sadie. 'Here's my wish: to restore the well, open a tea room, and live a long and happy life.'

'That's three wishes, you cheat.'

'You know what I mean.'

Martha sighed. 'When you really start thinking about wishes, they get very complicated, don't they?'

Angela grunted. 'That's why it's best left to the young and foolish.'

'But the young only ever want fame and fortune these days,' remarked Sadie. 'All they can think of is money. There's a few in Creighton Mere I can think of.'

'She means Nigel Carson and co,' explained Angela. The barmaid had stopped by to collect some empty glasses and Angela greeted her warmly. 'Lucy! How are our resident gold-diggers?'

Lucy smiled and winked. 'That's Mr Carson and friends to you, Angela.'

Angela adopted a mock deferential attitude. 'Mr Carson! How is the slimy toad, anyway? Rich beyond his wildest dreams yet?'

'Are there people here looking for the well treasure?' Martha asked, surprised.

'Nigel Carson and his university chums,' Sadie explained. 'At least, that's what we think they're up to. No one really knows. They say they're inspecting the village for a tour guide. Load of old tosh if you ask me, because they haven't once asked us about the well.'

'We prefer to think they're after the treasure,' Angela smiled. 'Makes things more interesting. Sad bunch, aren't we?'

'Sounds like fun, either way,' Martha said. Lucy's gaze rested on the Doctor for a long moment, but he was, of course, oblivious. Martha shuffled a little closer to him on the bench seat anyway, just to be sure.

'I don't think they've struck gold yet, anyway,' laughed Lucy. 'Here they come now!' She collected up the last dead glass and headed back to the bar.

Three men had entered the pub. The first, presumably Nigel Carson, was a smooth-looking guy in expensive clothes. He had dark hair swept back from a long, arrogant face and cold, grey eyes.

The other two were a strange pair. One was thin, rather bookish, with steel-rimmed glasses and with a laptop under one arm. The other was a much taller, broader man with untidy blond hair and a slightly broken nose. Martha immediately warmed to him when he looked around the pub, saw her, and smiled. He had very gentle blue eyes.

'Evening, Mr Carson!' Angela called across the pub, raising her glass. 'How's the tour guide going?'

He sneered back at her. 'We can't find anything to say about this place that won't put most people off.'

'Ouch,' Sadie said.

Nigel Carson sauntered over and looked down his nose at the four of them. 'You may be glad to know that we won't be here much longer,' he said. There was a sardonic twist to his smile. 'I think we're very nearly done.'

'You mean you've found the treasure already?' the Doctor asked innocently.

Nigel regarded him coolly. 'And who are you?'

'I'm the Doctor and this is my friend Martha. Pleased to meet you. How's the tunnel going?'

Angela and Sadie both spluttered and Martha struggled not to laugh. The look on Nigel's face was priceless – momentary panic, followed by fear and then anger. Raw nerve touched.

'I don't know what you're talking about,' Nigel replied eventually.

'Aww, c'mon. Don't be embarrassed,' said the Doctor. 'How else are you going to reach the treasure? You can't go down the well – it's blocked off with an iron grille, I've seen it. And it would be pretty obvious, let's face it, if you were going up and down the well-shaft right in front of everyone all the time. The whole village would know what you were up to. So, there must be a tunnel.'

'I said I don't know what you're talking about.'

'Yes, you do! The tunnel. How long have you been digging? Must be ages if there's only the three of you.' The Doctor sat back and folded his arms, smiling. 'Or rather two of you. You haven't been doing any digging, but you're friends have – I can see the dirt under their fingernails.'

Instantly, both Ben Seddon and Duncan Goode looked at their fingernails. Nigel glared at them both with a hiss of annoyance. 'You idiots.'

Then he turned on his heel and headed for the bar.

'Come on,' said Ben, pulling Duncan's arm.

'OK,' Duncan hesitated and smiled at Martha. 'Catch you later?'

Martha smiled back and waved her fingers.

'He's the only decent one,' whispered Angela loudly as they watched them go. 'Nice eyes, nice bum, and not as thick as he looks, either. No idea what he's doing with an oily snake like Nigel Carson.'

'Of course,' said Sadie, 'if you really want to know about the treasure, you should ask Barney Hackett.'

'Who's he?' asked the Doctor.

'The local tramp,' Angela said. 'I think you said you met him on the way into the village?'

'Ah.' The Doctor nodded. 'The one who wanted to warn us about nothing in particular.'

'Actually,' Sadie said, 'I think he's just a lonely old man, and a bit of an eccentric.'

Martha raised an eyebrow at this.

'No, really. He's harmless, just a bit grumpy.'

'And there's a hygiene issue,' Angela added with a loud sniff.

'Yes, well, be that as it may, Barney Hackett's lived around here all his life, and he probably knows everything. He does fancy himself a bit of an expert on the local legends.'

'Is that so?' said the Doctor thoughtfully. 'You know, I wouldn't mind another chat with Old Barney.'

FOUR

Nigel and Ben found a place to sit down and sent Duncan to the bar. Ben opened up his laptop. 'Look,' he said, turning the computer so that Nigel could see the screen as well. There was a CG schematic of the well-shaft going deep underground, and a tunnel heading towards the base at a shallow angle. 'That's the original tunnel. We've made another five metres. By my calculations there must only be another five metres to go – possibly even less, if we're lucky.'

Nigel licked his lips. 'So close…' he murmured. He stared at the laptop image and cursed softly.

'What's the matter?'

Nigel frowned. 'I didn't like that Doctor. How can he know what we're doing here?'

'Guesswork,' said Ben. 'That's how most people know.'

'What do you mean?'

'They may be everyday country folk around here, Nigel,

but they're not daft. They've probably got a pretty shrewd idea what we're up to. But don't worry about it. Whoever that Doctor is, he can't know for sure.'

'He does know,' Nigel insisted darkly. 'They all know. Even the old tramp outside knew. Someone's blabbed.'

This time Ben frowned. 'But no one else knows... Oh. I see.' He followed Nigel's sharp gaze, and saw Duncan leaning against the bar, laughing at something with Lucy. 'You don't think...?'

'Duncan's let the cat out of the bag,' snarled Nigel. 'It's the only explanation.'

Ben shook his head. 'I don't believe it.'

Nigel leaned forward and lowered his voice even further. 'If push comes to shove, Ben, we may have to cut him out of the deal. I'm not carrying freeloaders.'

'But... But it's Duncan. He's been in on this right from the start.'

'Doesn't mean he has to be in on it right at the end.' Nigel looked deep into Ben's eyes. 'We're talking about more than just money, here, Ben.'

'What do you mean? I thought the idea was we found the treasure and split it equally.'

'The damned treasure doesn't matter.'

Ben scratched his head. 'I don't know what you mean. We are in this for the money, aren't we?'

'Of course we are,' Nigel agreed after a second's hesitation. 'But what does that treasure mean to you, Ben? What does it actually mean?'

Ben shrugged. 'Money. Wealth. The chance to pay off my overdraft, for one thing. I don't suppose I'll know for sure until we find out what's really down there, and what it's worth.'

Nigel looked pityingly at him. 'I'll tell you what's down there. Power.'

'That's one way of looking at it I suppose.' Ben shifted uncomfortably and glanced at the bar where his old college chum was paying for their drinks. 'But Duncan has worked hard on this, Nigel. I know he doesn't take it as seriously as you'd like, but we really wouldn't be anywhere near where we are without him.'

'I don't doubt it. But at the end of the day muscle is muscle. It can be replaced.' Nigel sat back and watched Duncan's broad back through hooded eyes. Then he seemed to reach a decision. 'Still, that won't really matter now – we're close enough. We can keep Duncan on until we get the treasure and then…'

'Then what?'

Nigel smiled. 'Cut him out, of course.'

Angela was telling Martha all about the plans to fit a brand new windlass to the well the next day; it was all 'jolly exciting' according to Angela, which was the first time Martha had ever heard anyone say that and not mean it as a joke. She smiled delightedly and Angela took this to mean she found the whole prospect fascinating. 'You really should come and take a look tomorrow,' she insisted.

'Thanks, I will,' Martha promised, not sure if this was true or not. She could be halfway across the galaxy by then, or sightseeing in the Palaeozoic Era. Instinctively she turned to the Doctor to check.

Only to find that the Doctor had vanished.

'Your friend left a few minutes ago,' Sadie told her. 'He said he'd see you outside. I think he's gone looking for Barney Hackett.'

'Oh. Where's he likely to be?'

Sadie pulled a face. 'Try the well – this time of the day, he usually visits it to make a wish.'

'Thanks.' Martha grabbed her jacket and said cheerio to Angela and Sadie, promising to see them the next day. She hoped they didn't see her fingers crossed. She hurried towards the exit and ran straight into Duncan Goode, who was carrying drinks from the bar.

'Whoops!'

'Oh, sorry,' gasped Martha. 'Didn't see you there!'

He smiled. 'Well, I'm big enough.'

'Yes, you certainly are. Well, sorry and everything. Again.'

'Don't apologise. It was my pleasure, really.' He caught sight of her coat. 'Oh. Going so soon?'

Martha shrugged. 'I'm looking for my friend.'

'I could be your friend. Name's Duncan, Duncan Goode. Sorry, can't shake… you know.' He held up the three drinks he was holding together in his large hands.

Martha smiled. 'Nice to meet you, Duncan. I'm Martha Jones. Look, I'm in a bit of a rush…'

'Wait! I haven't told you about my wish…'

'What wish?'

'My wish – in the wishing well. It really works, see.'

'Yeah?'

'Absolutely. I came here a lonely man. I wished for a

friend – a lovely, dark-eyed friend of the opposite gender, to be precise. And look what happened!'

Martha smiled. She had to admire his nerve. 'Not just now, tiger…'

'Hey – don't judge a banana by its skin.'

'Pardon?'

'Listen, I may look gormless but I played rugby for my University's First XV. Second row – hence the nose.' Duncan briefly looked cross-eyed at his own, slightly crooked nose. 'Occupational hazard but good character-building stuff, so they tell me.'

'All right. So what's a bright boy like you doing with someone like Nigel Carson?'

Duncan shrugged. 'I just owe him a favour, that's all. And it's just a bit of fun anyway. But he's very intense. He can't help it – poor bloke's never even held a rugby ball, so what does he know?'

Martha smiled. 'Well, exactly.'

'Right. Look, you're welcome to join us for a drink anyway…' Duncan jerked his head at the far side of the pub where Nigel Carson and Ben Seddon were waiting.

When Martha glanced at them she saw they were glaring icily at her and Duncan. That immediately annoyed her. 'Do you know, I'd love to… but I really must see the Doctor first.'

Duncan frowned. 'Nothing serious, I hope…?'

'What? Oh, no, not that kind of doctor. It's my friend. He asked me to catch him up.' There was an embarrassing pause as the two of them looked uncertainly at each other, waiting to see who would speak next. 'Well, I'd better be going,' Martha said at last.

Duncan simply smiled at her. 'OK.'

Duncan put the drinks down on the table, spilling one of the pints slightly. 'Whoops. I'll have that one.'

'What were you talking to her about?' asked Nigel sharply.

'Who? Martha?'

'Yes.'

'Nothing.' Duncan took his seat. 'She just bumped into me. I asked her if she wanted to join us for a drink, that's all.'

'What?' Nigel snapped. 'Are you terminally thick? What do you want to ask her that for?'

Duncan looked over to where Martha was just disappearing through the door. 'Well… I quite like her.'

'In case you've forgotten, Duncan, we're not here to fraternise with the locals.'

'I don't think she's a local.'

'I don't care! She's with that Doctor, isn't she?'

'I suppose so.'

'He's trouble,' Nigel said bluntly. 'I can tell. He might be from the council. That well could be a listed building or something. Those stupid old women, the ones who want to refurbish the thing, they've probably called him in as a consultant or something. The girl's probably his partner. I don't want you to have anything to do with them again, clear?'

Duncan sipped his pint and shrugged. 'All right, keep your knickers on.'

Nigel took a deep breath and forced himself to relax. 'Anyway, we're nearly finished here. By tomorrow lunchtime you could be one of the three richest men in the country. Ben and myself being the other two, of course. You'll be fighting off girls like her with a stick.'

Duncan laughed softly. 'Maybe I will. But I won't believe it until I actually see the treasure. My mum always told me never to count my chickens before they're hatched.'

Ben tapped his computer. 'I've checked our progress. By my reckoning, this particular chicken will be hatched by tomorrow teatime. That's if we start at nine o'clock sharp. It's a full day's digging, but we're very nearly there.'

Nigel rubbed his hands together. 'Gentlemen! A toast…' He raised his glass. 'I give you the future – specifically, tomorrow!'

'Here's to the treasure!' said Ben happily.

'Power,' said Nigel.

FIVE

Martha found the Doctor standing in front of the well. 'Come to make a wish?' she asked.

He shook his head. 'Nah. I can never think of what to wish for. Well, no, I can, actually: lots of things. Too many things. I wouldn't know where to begin.'

'Gets complicated, doesn't it?' Martha hugged herself for warmth. The evening had turned chilly. 'So what's up, then? Come on, you can tell me: I'm nearly a doctor.'

He smiled. 'I just needed some fresh air, that's all.'

'What, you?'

'It's the dandelion and burdock. Goes straight to my head, always does.'

'It's the well, isn't it?'

'Something's not right, Martha.' He walked slowly towards the well, as if it was some kind of slumbering beast.

Martha joined him, peering over the parapet into the

dark depths. There was a cold, strange odour rising from it, as if something had fallen down it and died. With a shiver she thought of Sadie Brown's story about the highwayman. 'You think it's something to do with that treasure?'

'Possibly. It's interesting, because wells are traditionally places of power. They're frequently holy places – the name Holywell crops up all over the place, for instance. And they are often thought to be guarded by spirits – that's how wishing wells started. People would come to get some water and offer up a prayer or a coin in return. Sometimes they'd ask the spirit of the well to grant a wish.'

'D'you think there's a spirit in this well?' Martha leaned over the wall and peered down.

'Difficult to say.' The Doctor looked at her with one of his wry smiles. 'Sometimes the wells weren't guarded by a benign spirit – they were guarded by a monster.'

'Well, I don't think there's any monster down here,' said Martha, her voice echoing down into the darkness of the well. It was dusk, and she couldn't really see a thing, but the well appeared to be empty.

'Are you sure?' said a dry, old voice behind her.

Martha gasped and looked up. Standing very close to her was an old man with dark eyes framed by a tangle of dirty grey hair. 'Oh, it's you!' she said. 'You really made me jump!'

'It's Mr Hackett, isn't it?' said the Doctor brightly.

The man frowned at him. 'How do you know my name? I don't know yours!'

'It's all right,' Martha smiled. 'Someone told us you'd be here. But we haven't been properly introduced, have we?

I'm Martha Jones. How do you do?' She held out her hand, but Barney Hackett just stared at it as if he'd never seen a hand before. But this didn't put Martha off; she'd done enough training hours in A&E to know how often the elderly and confused just needed a quiet chat and a smile to help them along.

'I hear you're quite an authority on this well,' said the Doctor.

Barney glared at him. 'Who told you that?'

'Angela Hook.'

'She ought to know better, that one.' Barney sniffed loudly and wiped his nose on the sleeve of his parka. 'An' she ought to leave the well alone. It isn't safe.'

'Why?' asked Martha.

Barney looked at her as if the answer was obvious. 'People can fall down a well like that!'

'Really?'

'Yes – like Tommy.'

'Tommy?'

'Yes! He fell down the well only six months ago.'

'You're kidding!' Martha was shocked. 'Someone fell down there six months ago? How? What happened?'

'Tommy was just walkin' around the wall,' said Barney, regarding the stonework sadly. 'I think he heard something inside – I don't know what, but he kept peerin' down, down into the shadows. Then he just... fell in.'

'But there's a metal grille – look,' Martha said, pointing. 'That's been there years by the looks of it. How could anyone fall down?'

'Well, if they're small enough...'

Martha looked again at the bars criss-crossing the well-shaft. 'Small enough?'

'Tommy was just a normal-sized cat, you see.'

'Ah.' Martha looked back down at the thick metal grille. The gaps between the bars were certainly wide enough for a cat to slip through. She swallowed hard. What a way to go. 'I'm sorry,' she said to Barney. 'I'm really sorry. It must have been awful.'

'Oh, it's all right, love,' said Barney. 'He can't get out, but he still calls up to me every so often.'

'But I thought you said he fell down six months ago.'

'That's right.'

'But how can he have survived that long? He'd starve to death.'

'I know,' Barney said with a wet smile. 'But he still calls up to me.'

'Brrr,' said Angela. 'Look, I've got goose bumps!'

Sadie looked at the arm held out for her to inspect and pulled a face. 'It's pretty warm in here.'

'Yes, I know. It's like something walked over my grave.'

Now Sadie gave a shudder. 'Ugh. I hate that expression. What on earth can it mean?'

Angela gave a snort of laughter. 'Listen to me, I'm talking like Old Barney now.'

'Oh, I wonder if Martha and the Doctor have managed to find him?'

'I'd imagine so.' Angela sipped her beer, considering. 'Odd couple, weren't they?'

'I thought you said they were tourists?'

'I'm starting to wonder. They seemed very interested in the well.'

'Barney will tell them a few good stories.'

Angela frowned. 'That's what I'm afraid of. He'll fill their heads with all sorts of rubbish about the treasure. Oh, and that ridiculous story about his flipping cat!'

'Miaow!' said Sadie and they both laughed.

'No, but seriously,' Angela said eventually, 'you know what Barney's like. He can be a bit strange when he's talking about the well.'

'He's a bit strange at the best of times. But we did warn them, so stop worrying.' Sadie tapped the bundle of dog-eared notes on the table. 'Anyway, we're supposed to be checking over these plans for the windlass installation. Tomorrow's the big day, remember.'

'How could I forget? No doubt our lord and master will be paying us a visit. Henry Gaskin won't waste a chance like this to come and spoil our fun.'

'Oh, go on with you,' Sadie nudged her friend. 'You're looking forward to it really!'

'Don't even joke about it! If that unctuous toad dares to come close enough I'll biff him on the nose and to hell with the consequences.'

On the far side of the pub, Nigel Carson finished his drink and told the others to turn in for the night. 'I want you up early tomorrow,' he said tersely. 'Big day. Let's crack it and get out of this place for good.'

Ben and Duncan nodded. In truth they were both tired and the prospect of sleep was enough to make them leave without complaint. They finished their drinks and headed for their rooms. Nigel watched them go, and then his gaze settled on Angela Hook and Sadie Brown. They were still sitting in their alcove, huddled over a pile of papers and plans for their beloved wishing well.

He wondered where the Doctor and his friend had gone.

Abruptly concerned, Nigel went quickly to his room. It was at the top of a narrow flight of stairs, right at the front of the pub. It had a wardrobe, a TV and a single bed. There was a desk in front of a small window that overlooked the village green. It had a clear view of the well.

Nigel locked the door of his room and went straight to the window. He didn't turn on the light, because he didn't want to be seen. He pulled back the curtain and looked out. It was getting dark now, but there was plenty of moonlight.

The Doctor and his friend were standing by the well. They were talking to someone else – a familiar-looking old man. Barney Hackett.

Nigel watched the three of them for a full minute before he took the stone out of his pocket.

The blood raced through his veins as he sat down at the desk and took hold of the stone. He could already hear it whispering to him, urging him to take action. It had led him here to the village, to the well, all the way to the treasure. It had guided him and urged him and cajoled and, yes, even punished him. But now it was nearly over.

He wouldn't let anything jeopardise his work here. Certainly not some interfering busybody.

'What should I do?'

-*no one must interfere*-

'How can I stop him?'

-*i will stop him*-

Nigel allowed the chilly fingers to caress his mind, letting them gently search for a way into his innermost feelings, his deepest sense of self. He thought about the Doctor. The fingers probed his thoughts… touched… suddenly gripped. He had to stop himself from crying out loud. It had been an almost instinctive reaction, a reflex, as if the Doctor represented some kind of threat that was even greater than he had first realised.

-*look at him*-

Nigel's eyes snapped open, black and blood-rimmed, and he stared across the village at the Doctor and his friend.

-*watch*-

And Nigel knew then, beyond all doubt, that there could only be one option.

The Doctor had to die.

SIX

The Doctor, Martha and Barney Hackett were all looking down into the black depths of the well.

'I can't hear anything,' said Martha. She glanced at the Doctor, who just shrugged.

'Well, he don't call up all the time,' Barney said. 'Otherwise he'd lose his voice, wouldn't he?'

'What does it sound like?' Martha asked.

'Like a cat of course. Sort of yowling noise. I think he misses me…'

The Doctor straightened and scratched the back of his neck. 'Well, he's not saying anything now.'

Martha looked at him and rolled her eyes. Barney Hackett was probably a bit daft, not to mention rather drunk. She could smell the booze on his breath. It was one thing humouring him, but this was getting silly.

'Tell us about the legend,' the Doctor said. 'The one about the highwayman and the treasure.'

Barney Hackett sniffed loudly. 'Some say it were Jack the Lad himself…'

'Jack the Lad?' smiled Martha.

'Jack Shepherd, highwayman,' explained the Doctor. 'Caused quite a stir in Regency times. Tall, thin, cool as a cucumber. Your mother would have hated him. It's where the term "Jack the Lad" comes from.'

'… but it weren't him, really,' Barney continued. 'No one knows who it was, but let's say 'is name were Joe, an' he were on the run from the law. He'd stole gold an' jewels worth a king's ransom from the Duke o' York by all accounts an' they'd set the Bailiffs after him. Now Joe had already lost his horse, 'cos it fell lame a mile out from Buxton an' he used his last bullet to put the poor animal out of its misery. But then he were on foot, see, with the sound of gallopin' hooves close behind. If the Bailiffs caught him he'd be 'anged for sure. So he had to find somewhere to hide an' quick.'

He was a good storyteller, Martha thought. She smiled and leaned in closer as Barney lowered his voice dramatically. 'Joe came right through Creighton Mere with the militia hot on his heels. He took one look at the well an' knew what had to be done. He tossed the bags o' loot down and then climbed over the wall. Carefully, he lowered himself down and hung on by his fingertips inside the well.

'The militia arrived a minute later. The place was deserted. The captain rode his horse right around the village but they couldn't find old Joe. Not until a dog trotted up to the well and started barkin' loud enough to raise the dead, anyways. Suspicious, the captain checked the well and found Joe hangin' inside, holdin' on for dear life. His arms must've been gettin' tired an' he would hardly be able to feel his fingers any more. He'd hoped the horsemen would've ridden right through the village an' left him be. But when he heard the dog bark he knew the game was up. He looked up an' saw the captain of the militia looking right down at him, a cruel smile on his face.

'Well, what was Joe to do? He'd led the Bailiffs a merry old race all the way from Leeds. He'd dropped the treasure down the well, and there was no hope of gettin' it back now. All he could do was plead for his life. But how was he to do that? What could he bargain with – him in that position, danglin' from his fingertips?' Barney leaned back and smiled. 'Well, Joe told the captain that he'd dumped the loot in the woods, an' if he pulled him up out of the well he'd show him where it was hid. Then it could be returned to the Duke, or else the captain and Joe could split the takings between 'em and call it quits. Most of the lawmen were crooked in those days anyway, so it were a perfectly reasonable suggestion.'

Martha was captivated. 'So what happened?'

'The captain wanted the treasure for himself of course. They always do – the greed of men knows no bounds. But he'd guessed by now that Joe had already dropped it down the well. So he leaned over and, looking Joe right in the eyes, plucked his fingertips off the wall one by one.'

Martha swallowed.

'They say he let out a terrible scream as he fell,' Barney continued. 'A scream that carried on an' on until they couldn't hear it no more – as if Joe had fallen all the way to Hell itself.'

'Well,' said Martha, feeling slightly ill now. 'That's quite a story.'

'Oh, it doesn't end there, love,' said Barney with a gleam in his eye.

'I had a feeling you were going to say that,' said the Doctor.

Barney just smiled. 'Joe drowned along with his loot, but his bones never did rest easy. He'd sworn vengeance on the greed of men as he fell to his death, a vow that he never gave up. The next time the captain came to the village, which was a good ten years later, when he were newly married an' was on leave, he stayed at the inn overnight. Joe was waitin' for him, though. That night he climbed up out of the well, found the captain an' his bride, and murdered 'em in their beds…'

'All right,' said Martha after a pause, 'now it's just getting silly.'

'Don't scoff, love,' warned the old man with a frown. 'It don't do to scoff about these things.'

'Did Joe ever kill again?' asked the Doctor blandly. Martha could hardly believe her ears. Surely the Doctor, of all people, couldn't be taken in by this lurid tale of revenge from beyond the grave?

'Oh yes,' Barney replied eagerly. 'Many a time have Joe's cold, wet fingers closed around the throat of some poor wretch…'

'Now I know you're having us on,' laughed Martha. '"Cold , wet fingers"?'

'You really don't believe me?'

'No,' said Martha. 'I really don't. Doctor?' She threw him a challenging look.

The Doctor opened his mouth to reply and then closed it again, as if reconsidering. He blew out his cheeks and raised his eyebrows. Finally he stuffed his hands into his pockets and said, 'Well…'

'Oh shut *up*,' Martha said, slapping him lightly on the arm.

'I was just going to say,' the Doctor continued, turning to look at the well, 'that there's something strange going on here and it's connected with this well. I don't know exactly what it is yet—'

'A dead highwayman with cold wet hands?' Martha wondered drily.

'—but I intend to find out.'

'It's nothing but old wives' tales,' insisted Martha. 'You heard what Angela and Sadie said. People love this kind of stuff. They can use it on the tourists.'

'Wait a minute, Martha.' The Doctor turned back to Barney. 'You said something before about the greed of men… What did you mean?'

Barney Hackett said nothing. He was staring at the Doctor with a strange look in his rheumy eyes.

'Barney?'

The Doctor and Martha looked at him, waiting for a response, but none came. He stared back at the Doctor, his eyes wide and his mouth hanging open.

'Barney?' asked Martha. 'Are you OK?'

A thin strand of saliva ran from the old man's mouth as

he stood, unmoving. Then his eyes rolled up into his head, showing only the whites, and a gurgle of pain welled up from his throat.

Instantly Martha moved forward to catch him. 'He's having some sort of fit!'

'Don't touch him!' yelled the Doctor, grabbing Martha's hand and yanking her back. 'Look!'

A strange green light was shining from Barney Hackett's open mouth. It flickered briefly and then a thin spark leapt out, like a fluorescent green tongue, and Martha jumped back with a shout of alarm.

The light faded, but worse was to come. The old man let out an unearthly howl as his teeth seemed to move in his mouth, extending and pushing outwards like thin grey spikes from between his lips. He raised his hands and the fingers grew into long, bony sticks. Suddenly, with an unnatural crunch of breaking bones, long spines erupted from his flesh, emerging through his clothes like knitting needles.

'What's happening to him?' gasped Martha as Barney staggered backwards. The spines were all moving, waving like the antennae of a giant cockroach, probing the air around them. The old man – hardly recognisable now – fell back and his heels drummed on the grass as the terrible metamorphosis continued. A piercing shriek of pain died on the night air as the writhing mass of twiggy legs and arms and spines looked up at the Doctor and Martha through terrified eyes.

'What is it?' Martha demanded as the Doctor produced his sonic screwdriver. 'What is he? Some kind of alien?'

The Doctor quickly scanned the creature with the screwdriver. 'He's as human as you are,' he said. 'Or he was…'

A crackling green light covered Barney's body like a sheet. The Doctor said, 'His molecular structure can't cope with the accelerated mutation… it's going to collapse!'

And with a final, deathly sigh, whatever was left of Barney Hackett turned grey, and then black, and tiny cracks spread over the remains of his body like a swarm of insects. The ashes broke into flakes of dead tissue, falling in on themselves until the chill evening wind blew them away. In seconds there was nothing left of him except a patch of grey dust in the grass.

Martha backed away, feeling sick and weak, until she came up against the well. 'It's like he never even existed…'

'No.' The Doctor fixed her with a burning stare. 'He *existed* all right – he was every bit as much alive as you or me. Something did this to him – something killed him!'

'But… what? What could have done that?' A horrible thought suddenly hit Martha. 'Something that wanted to stop him speaking to us?'

The Doctor circled the faint patch of dust, his features solemn. 'I don't know. His entire physiognomy was altered, right down to the molecular level. But it happened too quickly.'

'Meaning what?'

'The change was too drastic, too sudden. His atomic structure couldn't cope with it and just collapsed. Well, you saw it happen. But whether that was intentional or not, I just don't know.'

'You mean something could have done that to him accidentally?'

'It's impossible to say.' The Doctor looked at the well, and Martha pushed herself hurriedly away from it.

'But how…?'

The Doctor shrugged. 'Did you see that green glow? That's some kind of telekinetic force field – mental energy reacting with the visible spectrum…' He rubbed his chin, lost in thought. 'But where from? And why?'

'We should tell the others,' said Martha, starting for the pub, but the Doctor caught her hand and held her gently back.

'We don't know what's happened here yet, not really,' he said. 'And what could we tell them? That Barney Hackett's just turned to dust before our very eyes?'

'Don't forget what happened before that – he turned into some kind… some kind of monster.'

'Do you think anyone will believe us?'

Martha's shoulders slumped. 'But… won't anyone miss him?'

'Of course. But he lived on his own, remember. No close family or friends to come looking for him.'

'But we can't just do nothing!'

'We will do something. But it's too late now. It's getting dark, and we can't do anything useful until tomorrow morning. We'll go back to the TARDIS. I can run some tests and then we'll come back first thing.'

Martha wasn't happy, and she looked back at the Drinking Hole, half expecting to find a small crowd of onlookers gathered outside. But there was no one. The village was deserted, only a few cars and Angela Hook's Land-Rover parked by the pub. Something moved in an upstairs window, and Martha glimpsed a curtain being drawn across the window of the pub's guest room. A shiver ran through her again and she suddenly felt drained.

'It's the telekinetic energy flux,' explained the Doctor. 'Whatever happened to Barney drew its power from all around us. You need sleep.'

Martha nodded and hooked her arm through the Doctor's as he led her away from the well. Some part of her brain registered a strange noise behind him, far away and lost in the depths of the approaching darkness: the sound of a sad, echoing cat's mew.

SEVEN

The next morning was overcast, as if the sun had simply decided not to bother. The Doctor seemed not to notice or care; he was up bright and early, full of energy. He'd changed his suit and plimsolls and ditched his tie, but otherwise it looked to Martha as if he'd been awake all night.

She found him standing by the TARDIS, watching the dawn as it crept across the dry-stone walls and rolling Derbyshire hills around them. Not far away was Creighton Mere. They could see the church from here.

'It doesn't seem right,' Martha said after a while. 'Just standing here, doing nothing. What happened to Barney was just awful.'

'I'm not doing nothing,' retorted the Doctor. 'I'm thinking.'

'What about?'

'Did you used to have a garden?'

Martha nodded, instantly transported back to the good times when her mum and dad had still been together: everyone laughing in the Jones' back garden as she tried to organise a game of tennis between herself and Tish. She was always Venus Williams, and Tish had to be Serena. Leo was ballboy, although he spent most of the time running away with the tennis ball, forcing his sisters to chase him. Happy times and places. 'Yes, we had a garden. Why?'

'Did you ever pick up one of the big stones in the damp corner of the garden and have a look underneath?'

'Ugh. No.'

'I always did,' said the Doctor wistfully. 'I always wanted to see what was lurking underneath, living in the darkness. Bugs and worms and things. You'd lift up the stone and they'd all be exposed, running away from the sudden light. Except the worms – they didn't run, of course. They just sort of squirmed and shrank.'

Martha shivered. 'And the point of all this?'

The Doctor nodded towards Creighton Mere. 'That's what this feels like. We're going to go down there and look under the stone. See what squirms.'

They reached the village in less than half an hour, and Martha appreciated the simple, old-fashioned beauty of the place far more this time, largely because she hadn't been rattling around inside an old Land-Rover on the way in.

It was busier this morning. There were a few cars passing through and some children waiting for the school bus. A man was walking his dog across the village green, and on the far side were Angela Hook and Sadie Brown, standing by the well. The Land-Rover was parked nearby, the rear door open to disgorge a pile of equipment including tool boxes, buckets and coiled ropes of various lengths.

'Morning!' said the Doctor brightly as they approached.

The ladies seemed delighted to see them again. 'You're just in time,' announced Angela. 'We're expecting delivery of the new windlass any minute. Fancy lending a hand?'

'Love to!'

Martha eyed the patch of grass where Barney Hackett had turned to dust the night before. There was no sign of his remains now.

'We're measuring up for the new roof, too,' said Sadie. 'It'll cost a bit, but we've got to have one.'

'Otherwise rainwater and debris will just fall down the shaft and spoil the water,' explained Angela.

'I thought you'd want rainwater,' said Martha, trying not to think about Barney.

'No, the water comes from underground springs,' Sadie said. 'Or at least it should. One of the things we still have to check is whether the well really has gone dry.'

'You said something yesterday about seismic movement,' the Doctor said.

'That's right. It makes the most sense.'

The Doctor shrugged. 'The best thing would be to go down and have a look.'

'Well, yes, obviously,' Angela agreed. 'But we can't do that – we're not fixed up for that kind of project yet.'

'Why not? You're getting a new windlass fitted. Once

the rope's in place someone could be lowered right down into the well.' The Doctor looked expectantly at them.

'You mean actually go down? One of us?'

'Well, I was thinking of me, actually.'

Angela and Sadie looked at one another. 'Do you mean that?'

He grinned and nodded.

'That would be marvellous,' said Angela, genuinely moved. 'We can't do it, after all. Too long in the tooth for that kind of lark – or that's what Sadie thinks anyway.'

'And I'm always right,' smiled Sadie.

The Doctor grinned. 'Then it looks like you're stuck with me.'

'Are you qualified?' asked Sadie. 'There are health and safety issues, after all. We don't want to be liable for anything.'

The Doctor produced the ID wallet containing his psychic paper. 'Ah! So you're from the Council's Heritage Department, eh?' said Angela, peering at it suspiciously. The Doctor flipped it shut and slid it back into his inside pocket without saying anything. 'I thought you were tourists.'

'Well, you know…' the Doctor replied, and rubbed the side of his long nose with a finger in the universal gesture for 'Don't tell anyone'.

The accompanying twinkle in his big, dark eyes did the trick, and Angela nodded immediately. 'Oh, yes, of course. Right-ho. Mum's the word!'

Martha bit her lip to stop herself smiling too broadly.

* * *

Ben and Duncan had got to work straight after breakfast. Moving to the head of the tunnel they quickly and expertly set up the lights and started to dig. Duncan took the lead with the pickaxe while Ben ferried the loose earth away in the wheelbarrow.

Nigel was impatient. They were so close. He stood behind them and watched, smoking cigarettes with trembling fingers. He couldn't hold them properly because of the gloves. That had prompted a question from Duncan: 'What's with the black gloves, Nigel? You look like a criminal mastermind this morning.'

Nigel had smiled humourlessly at the jibe. 'I *am* a criminal mastermind,' was all he said, but he was thinking of the damage to his hands: when he had finally let go of the stone last night, he had been left with painful blisters all over his fingers and the palms of his hand. The blisters had wept blood for a while, leaving him literally red-handed for the rest of the night. He had collapsed onto his bed, exhausted, the image of Barney Hackett's fatal transformation burned into his mind. But it was worse than that: the Doctor and his friend had seen it too, had watched as the old man turned to dust right in front of them… and yet they hadn't started screaming or running for help or even gone to tell anyone about the remarkable event they had just witnessed. They had talked to each other quietly for a few minutes and then left on foot.

And that had scared him more than Barney Hackett's unseemly death.

'What happened?' he had asked the stone in desperation. 'What did you do?'

-the human form is so weak-

For the first time Nigel detected an element of frustration in the stone. And the more frustrated the stone was, the more it hurt him.

-the transmutation could not be controlled-

Nigel had gritted his teeth through the pain. 'I don't know what you mean. I don't understand!'

-next time… next time-

Now there had been a sense of anticipation, of urgency. Nigel knew that he had to move fast. Part of him had wanted to go and wake Ben and Duncan there and then, to start digging straight away, but he was too tired himself. Communication with the stone had left him exhausted. He had to literally tear his hands from it and there had been blood. Eventually he had drifted into a disturbed sleep full of dark dreams.

The next day started well, however, with Ben showing him and Duncan a schematic diagram of the tunnel on his laptop. 'I've done some more calculations. Judging by the angle of descent and the information we have regarding the well depth, I think we're even closer to zero point than I thought. The treasure vault is right off the main shaft, according to the information we already have. Just about here, in fact.' He pointed to a spot on the screen. 'We're that close to breakthrough.'

It was the best possible news, and they set to work with renewed energy. Or at least Duncan and Ben set to work while Nigel watched. Ben had estimated another two hours' digging would bring them to the vault.

'Hurry up,' Nigel said, as Duncan paused to wipe the

sweat from his forehead after another half hour's toil. 'Another hour and we'll be the richest men in England.'

'Wait a second,' Ben said. 'What's this?'

Nigel turned back to find Ben kneeling down at the head of the tunnel, where Duncan had been clearing away a lot of loose shale and stones. There was something poking out of the earth, pale and shiny.

'Bring the light over here,' said Ben.

Duncan swung one of the lamps around so that the area was properly lit. Ben was already scraping away more soil, using his hands, until the buried object was revealed.

Nigel saw the teeth first, yellow and full of gaps, beneath a jagged hole and two empty sockets.

'It's a skull,' said Duncan.

Ben reeled back. 'Flipping heck!'

Working quickly, Duncan cleared away more stones and dirt until they could see the whole thing: a human skull, partly covered in dry, age-darkened skin stretched over the bone, still with wisps of brittle hair attached; then part of a shoulder blade and some ribs covered with rotted fabric.

'It's a body,' breathed Duncan. 'Someone's been buried here.'

'This far down?' Ben queried. 'Bit deep for a grave.'

'I don't like it,' said Duncan. 'We should tell the police.'

'Don't be stupid!' barked Nigel, his heart hammering with excitement as he stared into the empty sockets of the skull. 'Don't you realise what this is? It's the highwayman, you fools! The man who hid the treasure down the well! Don't you remember the story? He was thrown down the well after the gold.'

'Well, yes, I know,' Ben stammered. 'But I thought that was just a story.'

'Well now you know it was true!'

'We should still report it, I suppose,' Duncan said.

Nigel scoffed. 'What? D'you think the police are going to start an investigation into a murder that took place over two hundred years ago? Talk sense! This is nothing to do with anyone except us, do you understand?' Nigel clapped his gloved hands together and gestured towards the corpse. 'Don't you see what this means? We're right on track! If we've found the highwayman, then the treasure can't be far away! We're right on top of it! Now, dig! Go on, start digging again!'

'I don't know, Nigel,' Duncan insisted. 'It doesn't feel right.'

Nigel stared at Duncan with eyes full of greed. 'I said *start digging again!*'

The Doctor was peering down into the well again. 'How deep is it?' he asked.

'We don't actually know,' Sadie told him. She joined him at the parapet. 'It won't be easy going down there, Doctor. There's bound to be some decay, possibly subsidence... and undoubtedly a lot of vegetation – there will be weeds and so on clinging to the brickwork, maybe even tree roots breaking through.'

'Not to mention a blooming great metal grille across the top of it,' Angela added.

'It's supposed to prevent anything from falling down the well,' Sadie explained patiently.

The Doctor pulled a face. 'Yeah, it could do that,' he agreed. 'But have you thought it might also be there to stop anything *getting out?*'

'What?'

They all gasped as the Doctor suddenly vaulted over the parapet and landed on the grille. It shook under the impact of his trainers but held fast.

'Ye gods,' Angela roared. 'You've just taken ten years off me!'

The Doctor had dropped to his knees and was peering down through the metal bars, his nose practically touching the grille. 'Not enough light to see very far down,' he reported. 'But you're right about one thing – there are plenty of weeds down there, growing out of the brickwork.'

'What did you mean, stop anything getting out?' asked Sadie.

The Doctor's face popped up over the parapet, a picture of innocence. 'Did I really say that?'

A sudden commotion on the far side of the green snatched everyone's attention away. A long, gleaming Daimler had pulled up by the village cross and a large, rather angry man was getting out. He was dressed in a suit but wore an expensive Barbour coat over it. He had a bullet-shaped head with thin, receding hair the colour of old iron. As he strode across the green towards the well, Martha saw that his eyes, set deep beneath bristling grey brows, were glaring menacingly at Angela.

'What the devil's going on here?' he demanded haughtily.

'Uh-oh,' Sadie muttered. 'Here comes trouble.'

'Mind your own business, Henry,' said Angela shortly. 'Go on, clear off, you're not wanted here.'

Henry Gaskin snorted through his nose like a prize bull. 'You know perfectly well that this *is* my business,' he said. 'I have a duty of care to this village and you two are trampling all over – Great Scott, what the devil's he doing in there?'

They all turned to look at the Doctor, who was still standing on the grille. From this angle he appeared to be levitating at the top of the well. He raised a hand and waved his fingers at Gaskin.

'This is the Doctor,' explained Angela happily. 'He's from the council.'

'Is he, by God?'

'And he's come to help with the restoration work.'

Gaskin glowered at the Doctor. 'Get out of that well, you damn fool.'

The Doctor stared back. 'Say please.'

Gaskin reddened, and then his gaze quickly took in Martha too. He knew they were strangers to the village. 'Creighton Mere's well is a listed building,' he advised them. 'You'll need official authorisation to come anywhere near it.'

'Show him your ID, Doctor,' suggested Sadie.

'ID be damned,' snapped Gaskin. 'You'll all leave here this instant.'

'All right, here are my papers,' sighed the Doctor, clambering out of the well and reaching into his pocket.

'You have no papers,' Gaskin declared emphatically.

'The necessary documents can only be obtained from the local magistrate – and as I am the local magistrate, I can confirm that you have not, and will not, be granted any kind of permission to touch this well. Do I make myself clear? You have one hour.'

With a final black look at Angela, Gaskin turned on the heel of his shoe and marched back towards the Daimler. They watched as the car started up, pulled around the green and then disappeared in the direction of Gaskin Manor. The exhaust smoke was still in the air when Angela said, 'Confound that awful man. He never stops trying to interfere.'

'He did seem a bit upset,' the Doctor commented. 'Is he right about the well? Is it protected?'

'He's never provided any proof at all,' Angela said. 'I just don't believe him.'

Sadie said, 'Until he shows us evidence that there's any kind of preservation order on the well that could prevent us working on it, we're going to carry on.'

'Good for you,' said Martha. 'He's a right old misery guts, isn't he?'

Sadie smiled. 'Don't let all the bluster fool you. He's not so bad. He's done a lot for the village, really, and I think what he really resents is the fact that he's not involved in the well refurbishment.'

'Didn't anyone ask him?'

'It's complicated.' Sadie lowered her voice and glanced across at Angela, who was talking to the Doctor by the well. 'Angela and Henry go back a long way; there's a bit of a feud going on.'

'Why?'

'Well, only Angela can explain that. But it has something to do with her husband. Roger Hook was killed in a mountaineering accident in 1989. Henry Gaskin was with him, they were climbing together. So Roger died and Henry survived. I don't think Angela's ever forgiven him…'

Martha nodded, feeling sorry for her. Angela seemed like such a strong, cheerful old lady, but in reality she was a widow of nearly twenty years and every time she saw Henry Gaskin it just reminded her of the painful loss. It certainly explained Angela's bitterness towards Gaskin and clearly the dispute over the well was the perfect opportunity to express it.

'Right then,' said the Doctor, clapping his hands together in an effort to restore some purpose to the proceedings. 'First things first: before we can get the new winding gear installed, we need to remove the grille.'

'Won't be easy,' grunted Angela. 'The wretched thing's rusted into the brickwork.'

'Oh, I might have something that'll help,' the Doctor smiled casually, holding up his sonic screwdriver.

'That doesn't look especially useful, Doctor.'

He shook his head patiently. 'Don't be deceived by appearances, Angela. Some people think I don't look especially useful. Whereas in fact…' He clicked his tongue. 'Actually you might have a point, but let's see.'

Angela laughed uproariously at this. Martha watched her carefully, thinking that perhaps the Doctor reminded Angela of another energetic, enterprising young man she had known a long time ago.

EIGHT

The grille came away more easily than anyone could have hoped. The Doctor loosened the concrete around the edges with his sonic screwdriver, and a couple of burly young men helped lift the metal trellis free. They dumped it on the grass by the Land-Rover.

The burly young men were from a carpentry firm in Congleton, and they had brought the new windlass. It was made of treated oak and extremely heavy, although Sadie assured them the well's original uprights could take it. 'It's been made to measure,' she said, 'according to the plans and the engineer's report. It's perfect.'

The burly young men were happy enough to deliver the windlass, but they didn't like the idea of helping to fix it in place – at least until Martha walked around from the far side of the Land-Rover. Then they were only too pleased, stripping off their shirts and arguing about which of them was going to take the heavier end of the windlass. Martha smiled shyly at them, which only urged them to greater efforts, while Angela, Sadie and the Doctor all watched with amusement.

It took nearly an hour to install the spindle and the men were perspiring by the end of the job. They collected their shirts and then looked for Martha, who smiled warmly at them and linked her arm through the Doctor's. The men glowered at the tall, skinny geek in the tight suit and then clambered wearily back into the cab of their lorry. Everyone waved as the engine started and the lorry drove off in a cloud of black exhaust.

'Right then,' said Angela, clapping her hands in triumph. 'Let's put it to the test!'

'Already?' Sadie asked.

'Why not? At the very least it might help us see how deep the well is.'

The Doctor and Sadie installed the rope on the spindle, and then Martha wound it on. Her arms were aching by the time all one hundred feet was coiled around the windlass. Then it was simply a matter of attaching a bucket.

'You won't bring any water up, that's for sure,' cautioned Sadie. 'You may not even reach the bottom of the well – the bucket may get caught up in some of the vegetation.'

'Let's find out!' said Angela.

They wound the bucket down and slowly the rope uncoiled. Martha and the Doctor peered down the well-shaft but the bucket soon disappeared into the shadows.

'It's a deep one,' said the Doctor as the rope continued to play out. Eventually it went slack as the bucket came up against something.

'The bottom, do you think?' asked Angela.

'Can't tell. We must be seventy feet down already, though.'

Suddenly the rope went taut again, as the bucket dropped a little further.

'Hang on,' said Angela. 'It must have got caught on something, and now it's free.'

Then the rope began to play out again, the windlass spinning on its own.

'It's falling,' said Martha as the winch handle spun faster and faster.

The windlass whirred in its sockets and then suddenly jerked to a halt as the rope reached its end. A loud twanging emanated from the well-shaft as it drew as taut as a violin string.

'Wow, that's deep,' said Martha with a nervous laugh.

'Hang on, something's wrong.' The Doctor peered down the shaft. The rope was humming, a ruler-straight white line disappearing into the depths. 'It's being pulled!'

'What?' Martha ran to join him. 'How?'

Suddenly the windlass gave a loud crack and the uprights shuddered.

'It's going to break the spindle!' yelled Angela as the solid oak beam began to creak under the strain.

The Doctor pointed his sonic screwdriver at the rope and the tip glowed blue. The rope instantly unravelled and snapped, whipping like a headless snake as it was yanked down into the well.

Then silence.

'What was that all about?' wondered Angela quietly.

'Something's down there,' said Martha, her voice shaking slightly.

'Nonsense,' said Sadie. 'There can't be anything down there. Probably the bucket dislodged some loose brickwork from the shaft on the way down and the weight did the rest.'

The Doctor exchanged a glance with Martha and then said, 'There's only one way to find out.'

'What's that?'

He grinned at her. 'I'll have to go down and have a look myself!'

Ben and Duncan had uncovered the entire skeleton, much to Nigel's annoyance. He thought they were simply wasting time. 'Just dig!' he instructed them. 'You're practically through to the treasure chamber!'

Duncan looked up from the bones. 'We don't want to disturb the remains too much,' he said. 'This was a person, once, Nigel.'

'Well it's not a person now, is it? Leave it. Keep digging.'

'Look at him, though...' Ben indicated the exposed corpse. It was lying slightly on one side, legs pointing towards the end of the dig. There were some scraps of leather clinging to the feet, the remains of a pair of boots. The rest of his clothes were little more than pieces of material mixed with mud and stone, with the occasional bone sticking out whitely from the dirt. 'You can see that this is where he fell,' Ben continued, enthused by his amateur post-mortem. 'One leg is slightly bent and this arm – here – is outstretched...'

'Almost as if he was trying to get away from the treasure chamber,' said Duncan.

'Yeah – almost like he was crawling.'

'It's pretty sad, really,' Duncan remarked. 'He died down here all alone, probably terrified. Maybe there was a tunnel collapse and he suffocated to death.'

Ben looked up at the roof of the tunnel and swallowed. 'Doesn't bear thinking about, does it?'

'Exactly,' said Nigel. 'So let's get on with it.' He made a show of checking his watch. 'I estimate that we could have been rich beyond our wildest dreams almost fifteen minutes ago.'

Duncan got to his feet, wiping the mud from his jeans. 'All right, all right… We just wanted to give the poor fella a bit of respect, Nigel.'

'OK, fine, respect given.' Nigel picked up the shovel and handed it to Duncan. 'Now dig.'

'Uh oh,' said Sadie. 'Look who's coming…'

Martha and the Doctor looked up to see Henry Gaskin striding across the village green. This time his trousers were tucked into green wellington boots and a lively looking Border Collie was trotting alongside him. Angela immediately bristled, standing upright and squaring her shoulders.

'I've been on to the local council,' stated Gaskin without preamble. 'They haven't sent anyone here today.'

'Ah,' said the Doctor, 'that's because you asked the wrong council.'

'Wrong council? What are you blithering about, man?'

'We're from the Well Council.'

'Well Council?'

The Doctor smiled. 'All's well that ends well, that's our motto.'

'I've no time for impudence,' snapped Gaskin. 'You'd better leave before I call the police.'

'Hang on a minute,' said Martha, 'we're not doing any harm…'

'It's pointless arguing with him,' said Angela. 'He won't listen, he never does.'

'I'll listen if there's anything worth listening to,' Gaskin replied tartly. His dog was busily exploring the well, sniffing here and there at the equipment spread about. Gaskin's beady eyes alighted on the new windlass. 'What's that?'

'The new windlass,' said Sadie.

'You've no right.'

'Don't worry about it,' said the Doctor. 'All we need now is a new rope. Give us enough and we'll hang ourselves, no need for you to put yourself to any trouble.'

'The Doctor's going to go down the well,' Angela announced triumphantly. 'Spot inspection, on behalf of the Well Council.'

'Wishing Department,' smiled the Doctor genially.

'I absolutely forbid it,' Gaskin said. He gave the Doctor a very black look. 'I don't know what you're doing here, young man, but I'm calling a halt to it right now. I know the stories about this well – treasure and monsters and what have you. You lot are just trading on those stories for your own ends. There is no treasure and there are no monsters. Fact. Now I am asking you, once again, to stop what you are doing and leave.'

Angela stepped forward, hands dug deep into her camouflage jacket pockets. 'Now listen here, Henry. I've had just about enough of you trying to throw your weight around this village, and particularly this well. The truth is you have no business here, no authority, and there's nothing you can do to stop us. Sadie and I were voted onto the refurbishment committee by the village Residents' Association, and there's not a blind thing you can do about it. We're not after any treasure – frankly I don't even believe in it – but we do want this well properly restored and fit for use. If you don't want to help us with that, then at least don't try to hinder us.'

Gaskin met her gaze steadily for a long moment. The two of them stared at each other, as if each was willing the other to break the silence. Finally, in surprisingly gentle tones, Gaskin said, 'Very well, if that's your final word on the matter – I'll let you waste your time and money on a pointless exercise. It'll be your loss.' He turned to leave and then paused. 'But don't say I didn't warn you, Angela.'

And with that he strode off towards the manor, with the Collie dog at his heels.

Sadie clapped her hands. 'Oh, well done, Angela! Bravo! You were superb!'

'About time someone stood up to him,' muttered Angela. She seemed suddenly deflated, as if the confrontation had taken all the energy out of her.

Martha was frowning. 'But what was that all about at the end – what warning? What did he mean?'

'Don't take any notice, dear,' Angela said wearily. 'He's full of hot air, that one. He's just trying to frighten you.'

'Which is interesting,' the Doctor said quietly to Martha. 'We've heard all about the treasure and the highwayman and the well... but he's the first person to mention anything about monsters.'

NINE

The Doctor checked the last buckle on his harness and grinned at Martha. 'All set?'

'No,' said Martha, arms folded. Angela and Sadie were busy fitting a new rope to the windlass, having supplied the Doctor with the necessary equipment. Angela still had a lot of her ex-husband's climbing gear and had dashed home to fetch it. Now the Doctor wore a sort of mountaineer's belt fitted with leg-loops and various metal hooks over his own suit. 'Isn't there anything else we can do?' Martha asked eventually.

His expression grew more serious. 'Nothing – except just walk away. Go back to the TARDIS and leave. And we're not going to do that, are we?'

'No.'

'There's no point standing around up here wondering what's down there,' the Doctor told her as he fastened a karabiner to his climbing harness, 'when we can easily go down and just have a look.'

'But you saw what happened to the bucket,' Martha argued. 'It nearly broke the windlass.'

He shrugged. 'Sadie could be right, it could have been an accident.'

'You don't really believe that, do you?'

He didn't reply. He simply turned to Angela and asked, 'All set?'

She gave him the thumbs-up and demonstrated the winch and pulley system she had set up under the new windlass. 'It's a modern equivalent of a block and tackle,' she told them. 'Very simple to operate – it lets the rope out at a steady rate through this…' she rattled a steel handgrip through which the rope passed. There was a hand-operated lever attached so that it looked like an oversized bicycle grip and brake. 'If I keep the lever pressed the rope plays out. If I release the grip then it locks. Safe as houses.'

'This rope is a lightweight nylon mix used by mountaineers and potholers,' explained Sadie, holding up a length of bright blue cord which led back to a large drum. 'It's perfect for this kind of job.'

'You're certainly well prepared,' commented Martha, impressed.

'The secret of our success, dear.'

'We'll lower you down,' said Angela, as the new rope was attached to the Doctor's climbing harness. 'Take it slowly because we really don't know what you'll find – there could be partial collapse of the shaft wall, tree roots, undergrowth, anything. You'll need this, too.' She handed him a large torch. The Doctor switched it on and trained it on his other hand; even in broad daylight the beam looked powerful. There was a lanyard attached, which the Doctor hooked onto his belt.

'Take this as well,' Sadie said, handing him a compact radio. 'Walkie-talkie. You can stay in touch with us up here, and report back what you find. If there's the slightest problem, yell and we'll pull you up sharpish.'

'It'll be cold down there,' cautioned Angela. 'Don't you want to put something warmer on?'

The Doctor said he was fine as he was and then swung his long legs over the parapet of the well-shaft. Martha looked down into the inky depths and shivered. 'You will be careful, won't you?'

''Course I will,' he replied cheerily, as if he was never anything but. 'Don't worry, I'm only popping down for a quick look. I'll be back in five minutes.' He checked the rope by giving it a hard tug, and then looked at her. Again, there was that seriousness back in his dark eyes and Martha felt an intense pang of worry. 'Listen,' he said, quietly. 'If anything goes wrong – go and see Henry Gaskin.'

Martha frowned. 'What? Why him?'

But the Doctor had already swung himself off the wall and was dangling over the well-shaft. He swung gently to and fro, and Angela began to squeeze the winch grip. Slowly the rope began to move through the pulley hanging from the windlass and the Doctor was lowered into the well.

'Good luck!' Sadie called down after him. He looked up and grinned, already disappearing into the cool shadows. 'Be careful!'

After a very few seconds Martha saw the Doctor switch his torch on and a bright white beam stabbed into the shaft wall. She caught a glimpse of crumbling brickwork as the light swivelled erratically; the Doctor was beginning to turn on the rope. The torchlight described a complete circle and the last thing Martha saw of the Doctor was a brief glimpse of his long, pale face looking back up at her. Then he was submerged in a pool of darkness and all she could make out was the distant glow of the torch. He had been completely lost from sight in a remarkably short time.

She forced herself to look up at the winch. There was still an awful lot of rope on the drum to play out. He had a long way to go.

Duncan and Ben were working their way past a large rock embedded in the earth. It took several big hits with the pickaxe to split the thing, but eventually they were able to pull the broken pieces out and discard them. They were taking less care with the loosened soil now because they knew they were nearly at the end of things; there was no need to ferry it all back up to the entrance and keep everything tidy.

'Watch out for our friend,' said Ben, as Duncan threw a chunk of rock across the tunnel and narrowly missed the skeleton.

'Sorry, mate,' Duncan grinned at the skull. 'I wonder who he really was?'

'I told you, it was the highwayman,' said Nigel. He was leaning against the tunnel wall, hands on his knees, feeling very unwell. The others put it down to claustrophobia. He knew it was something far worse.

'I mean, what was his name?' wondered Duncan.

Ben said, 'We'll have to call him John Doe.'

'Nah, too American. He's English: Joe Bloggs.'

'Joe Bones, you mean.'

'Hah! Yeah, Joe Bones. Hello, Joe, nice to meet you!' Duncan bowed to the skeleton. 'Hey, Joe, you've lost a bit of weight.'

They laughed together, starting to feel a bit drunk on the prospect of being so close to the end. Treasure or not, they both wanted this digging over.

'Hey, look at this,' Duncan said, when they had calmed down a little. He was pointing at the cavity in the earth where the big rock had been. Immersed in the soil was a tangle of pale and fibrous vegetable matter. 'What's that?'

'Roots or something, I suppose,' said Ben.

'I'd have thought we were a bit far down for roots,' Duncan remarked. 'There aren't any trees near enough which could have a root system running this deep.'

Ben shrugged. 'I don't know. There could be some old growth down here, I suppose.' He bent down to have a closer look. The tendrils were so pale they were almost white, straggling through the soil like thin wires. 'It looks very pale – starved of sunlight. No photosynthesis. Probably dead.'

'Weird!' Duncan moved the torch closer and the roots almost seemed to glow. 'I've never seen anything like that before!'

'Come and have a look at this, Nigel,' said Ben, indicating

the remains of the white weed-like substances trailing through some of the soil and rock fragments. 'What do you make of it?'

'Nothing,' Nigel replied, hardly sparing it a glance. He sounded distracted. 'It's not treasure is it? That's all we're interested in…'

Duncan was watching Nigel closely. 'Hey, Nigel. You don't look well, you know.'

'I'm fine.'

Ben looked. 'Dunc's right. You look as white as a ghost. Why don't you go and have a sit down, let us carry on.'

By now Nigel was leaning weakly against the tunnel wall. 'I think I'm just tired. We're so close…'

Duncan rested a hand on his shoulder. 'Do what Ben says. Go and have a rest. We'll come back and get you the moment we find anything.'

'I-I don't know…' Nigel didn't look happy about it.

'We've got another couple of metres to go,' Ben assured him. 'It's not much but there's a lot of rock and it could take a little while longer. You can't stand here. You look like you're going to throw up any minute.'

'All right,' Nigel nodded. 'Call me the instant you find anything.'

'Will do.' Duncan patted him on the arm and Nigel walked slowly away, heading back up the tunnel.

Nigel stopped at the mouth of the tunnel and took several deep breaths. The climb back up the steep gradient had winded him but his whole body was tingling and there was a familiar stirring deep inside his head.

He felt in his coat pocket and took out the stone.

It was vibrating; just slightly, enough for him to feel it through his gloves. A sort of complacent hum, almost like the purring of a cat.

He raised it up so that he could look at it more closely. The surface had changed. And, even as he watched, the surface began to move – microscopically, almost as if a million tiny fragments were chasing each other around like insects. It made the stone appear almost fuzzy, or blurred. Nigel had once seen a termite mound disturbed; the number of insects that had poured out had formed a sort of living mass, a river of movement, and that's what the surface of the thing looked like now. It still felt solid in his hand, but he could see and feel the activity.

He wondered if the stone was as excited as he was.

'What's the matter?' Nigel asked. 'You've never done this before.'

-i must grow... i must feed-

'Nearly there,' he murmured soothingly. 'Nearly there...'

-hurry-

Tiny little fingers stood up from the surface of the stone, uncoiling and probing the air like worms. They waved blindly for a few moments, sliding over his fingers and hands, and then began to lash back and forth in a more feverish manner.

-i must grow-

Nigel smiled. 'Yes! I know... I know... we're so very close now...'

-it is not enough-

'I'm sorry, I don't understand…'

-you will never understand-

Suddenly, sharp, barbed spines dug into his hands and Nigel cried out in pain. He felt the blood welling from his palms and fingers, and, when he tried to let go of the stone, he found that it was impossible.

'What are you doing? You're hurting me!'

-i must feed and grow. the time of rising is near-

Nigel gasped in pain. 'I don't know what you mean—'

-i am ready-

'R-ready for what?'

-the rising-

He couldn't bear it any long, couldn't understand what was happening. The pain in his hands was intense, but nothing compared to the pain in his head. It felt as if the little barbs had reached all the way into his mind and were tearing through his brain tissue.

Nigel forgot all about Duncan and Ben, all about the treasure, everything. All he wanted to do now was get out and breathe fresh, clean air. He had to get away from here.

He had to get away from the stone.

But, try as he might, he couldn't get rid of it; he shook his hands but the stone held fast, digging its little fingers deeper into his flesh.

With a sob of fear, Nigel emerged into the blinding light of day and stumbled forward.

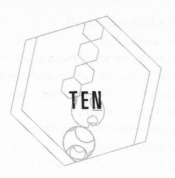

TEN

At the top of the well, Sadie was showing Martha how to use the walkie-talkie. 'This red light means it's on. That's the frequency – it's set to channel one. Press this switch when you speak, release it to listen.'

'Gotcha.'

They were looking down into the well, but all they could see was the blue rope disappearing into the darkness. Martha kept thinking she could see the distant glimmer of the Doctor's torch as it moved around the shaft, but she couldn't be sure.

She pressed the switch on the walkie-talkie. 'Doctor? Are you there?' She remembered the way people usually spoke on radio transceivers and added, 'Do you read me, over?'

The walkie-talkie crackled and then the Doctor's voice rang out loud and clear: 'Hello, Martha!'

She laughed with relief and pressed the switch again.

'We can't see you any more. What's it like down there?'

'Dark and cold,' came the reply with a crackle of static. 'There is a lot of vegetation down here, weeds and stuff, but you can tell Sadie the shaft wall is in pretty good condition so far.'

'That's great!'

'Hang on a…' the Doctor's voice faded briefly and then returned, '… to get through here. I'll need… hands to move it.'

'Didn't get that. Can you repeat, over?'

Crackle. 'Lots of weeds and… yes, probably brambles I think. I'll need both hands to move it so I can get past. Hold the rope a minute. I'll have to switch the walkie-talkie off. Over and out.'

The radio crackled and Martha looked at Angela. 'I heard,' she said, and stopped winding the rope out. 'He's doing well, isn't he?'

'I hope so,' Martha said. 'He has a knack of finding trouble, though.'

The Doctor spun slowly in the darkness, watching the light from his torch play over the shaft wall. There was a tangle of weeds and roots growing all over the old brickwork, and a big patch of brambles. The light gleamed briefly on the tips of some viciously sharp thorns.

With great care he pushed aside some of the thinner, more straggling branches, doing his best to avoid the thorns. The brambles grew more thickly below, almost like a barrier.

Craning his neck, the Doctor looked back up the well-shaft. It was very dark, but he could still see a coin-shaped white disc above him. The sky. It seemed alarmingly small and distant. But there was still a lot further to go; he had to carry on.

Steeling himself, he turned back to the matter at hand. He swung himself across the well and grabbed hold of one of the sturdier roots. It was growing out of the shaft wall, but the damage didn't look too bad. Nothing that couldn't be patched up once the vegetation was removed. He twisted around in his harness and shone the torch downwards. He could see a narrow gap through the bramble thicket. If he took it carefully, he could probably climb down right through it.

Beyond the brambles was nothing but impenetrable blackness. The torch beam was simply swallowed whole. He found the walkie-talkie and pressed the call switch. 'Hello up there…'

Martha's voice crackled faintly: 'Hi! Everything OK?'

'I've found a way through the worst of it. You can lower away.'

'Right! Lowering away…'

The rope hummed and the Doctor positioned himself so that he dropped through the clear way. The odd thorn snagged on his clothes, but otherwise he passed through without a hitch. The brambles closed over his head like a tangled ceiling as he descended into an altogether colder, damper darkness.

The Doctor shivered. It wasn't the cold so much as something else – a deathly atmosphere completely at odds with anything he had experienced on Earth before. It was as if in passing through the brambles he had passed into another world.

The torchlight picked out something else growing up the brickwork; a strange, fibrous growth which stayed close to the walls and was much paler than the vegetation he'd seen so far. Some of the stems looked oddly withered, meandering in a haphazard fashion with milk-white tendrils creeping between the narrow gaps around the bricks. There were other things down here, living things, moving in the torchlight: snails and beetles and spiders. When the light hit the snails, their translucent antennae shrank to nothing; the insects and the spiders scurried away into the cracks in the wall.

His walkie-talkie crackled and he jumped. Fumbling, he raised it to his lips. 'Hello?'

'Hello?' said Martha, holding the walkie-talkie in both hands. 'Hello? Doctor? Can you hear me, over?'

The only reply was white noise.

'I can't get anything out of it,' Martha said.

Sadie took the radio and fiddled with it, but the only sound was static now. 'He must've have passed out of range,' she said.

Martha turned to Angela. 'Do you think we should pull him back up now?'

'The rope's still going out,' Angela said, nodding at the brake. 'He's still descending.'

'I didn't think it would be this deep.'

'There's not much more to go now. We'll play it right out.'

* * *

The Doctor pulled a face at the useless walkie-talkie and slipped it back into his pocket. He didn't think he'd come far enough to be out of range. Perhaps something was interfering with the signal.

He was still descending, which was good. He didn't want Angela to panic and start hauling him back up too soon. There was still a lot to see.

He waved the torch around the walls. The snails recoiled and the spiders ran. There was a lot of the white weed here; in some places it grew so thickly the brickwork was completely obscured. Now there were lumps of it here and there, like a sudden growth of fungus, with spindly little twigs thrusting out like fingers groping in the darkness.

The Doctor reached out and touched the twigs. They were warm. He frowned, unable to decide if they were plant or animal in origin.

There was one particular patch where a number of thick, pallid branches had extended halfway across the shaft in a kind of fibrous web. It was almost as if the weed – or whatever it was – had grown around something. The Doctor took out his glasses and slipped them on for a closer look as he drew level.

He pointed the torch at the lumpy mass. There was definitely something inside the weed. Carefully he reached out and tugged at some of the fronds, and they came away quite easily. Beneath there was something small and round and dark. The light picked out a tiny face with matted fur and whiskers.

'Uh oh,' said the Doctor quietly.

The dead cat was almost overgrown with the weeds. The Doctor pulled some more fronds away, exposing the ginger ears and an old collar with a name tag. Squinting, he pulled the collar around until he could read the name on the little metal disc.

'Tommy,' read the Doctor. 'Barney Hackett's cat. So this is where you ended up, eh, puss?'

There was silence in the well-shaft as the Doctor stared sadly at the feline remains.

Then the cat's eyes snapped open and it mewed at him.

ELEVEN

'**D**id you hear that?' said Martha suddenly, waving a hand at Angela to stop her speaking.

'Listen!' Martha leaned right over the well, straining to hear.

'I can't hear anything,' said Sadie.

'Shush,' Angela ordered. 'What did it sound like, Martha?'

Martha swallowed. 'Well, I can't be sure... but...' She looked back up at the two women. 'Well, it sounded like a cat mewing.'

Sadie actually laughed. 'Oh, come on! Don't tell me Barney Hackett's been telling you his ghostly cat stories!'

Angela was smiling too. 'He still reckons his little Tommy's down there, calling back up to him...' She put a hand to her mouth and looked upwards, mimicking someone calling up a well-shaft. 'Miaow!'

'No, I'm serious,' Martha objected. 'Listen, I'm sure of it.'

They all listened but there was nothing.

'Pull him back up,' Martha instructed Angela.

'Don't be daft,' she said. 'He's nearly reached the end of the rope anyway.'

'I said pull the Doctor back up.'

Sadie put a hand on her arm. 'Martha, you're overreacting. It's just a story. Barney Hackett's cat fell down that well months ago. It's dead.'

'I know, he told me.' Martha ran a hand through her long black hair in exasperation. 'Listen, there's something you should know about Barney…'

They looked expectantly at her.

'We saw him last night, right here by the well…' Martha looked at the patch of grass where the old man had turned to dust. 'It was horrible.'

'He's always hanging around the well,' Angela said. 'In fact, I'm surprised he's not here now.'

'What do you mean, it was horrible?' asked Sadie with a frown.

Martha took a deep breath. 'Something happened here last night, something terrible. You've got to believe me, the Doctor could be in real danger. Pull him back up!'

Confused, but seeing the genuine fear in Martha's eyes, Angela released the handgrip on the winch. 'All right,' she said. 'I'll wind it back up…'

But the winch wouldn't budge. 'It's stuck,' she said.

Martha joined her and added her own strength, but the mechanism might as well have been carved from solid rock.

Angela reached across the well and touched the rope.

'Ye gods, it's as taut as a bow string,' she said. 'Something's pulling on it – hard!'

Martha looked back at the frozen windlass and then back down the well. 'What are we going to do? Doctor!'

The cat's eyes closed again, and for a long moment the Doctor just stared at it. When the animal still didn't move, the Doctor reached out to touch it. It was cold and stiff. There had been no life in the dry, cracked eyes. The thing was dead and had been for a long time. Or at least it should have been. What was keeping it going? The weed?

Something touched his leg and he aimed the torch down at his feet. There was a large mass of the white weed spread out below him like a gigantic cobweb stretched across the well-shaft. His plimsolls were touching some of the strands. He tried to pull his legs back up away from the tangled growth, but the uppermost fronds had somehow wound themselves around his feet. He kicked out but found the weed had got quite a grip.

'Not good,' he murmured. 'Not good at all.'

He shone the torchlight down and, to his mounting consternation, saw that the milky tendrils were actually moving, feeling their way over his ankles and up his shins. They crept under his trousers and over the material, increasing their grip.

Hurriedly he pulled out the walkie-talkie and pressed the transmit button. 'Hello? Martha? Can you hear me?'

There was nothing, not even static now. He shook the radio and tried again. 'Martha? Angela? Anyone?' With a hiss of annoyance he stowed the walkie-talkie again, but in doing so lost his grip on the torch and the lanyard slipped free of his belt. The beam of light whirled briefly as the torch fell and disappeared into the web below. For a moment the light shone directly upwards, illuminating the Doctor as he hung in the air like a puppet on a string. The weed had crawled up over his knees now, and was beginning to exert pressure – pulling him down.

And then the light faded. The Doctor couldn't tell if the torch had died or if it had fallen deeper into the morass below until the light was completely lost – but either way, it hardly mattered. Because suddenly the Doctor was plunged into complete and utter darkness. He couldn't see a thing.

And the weed was still pulling him down.

'It's working!' announced Angela suddenly as the winch rattled into life. 'It must have got caught on something again.'

Martha peered down the well, but she couldn't see anything. The walkie-talkie was useless. She tried calling down, but her voice just seemed to fall away into nothingness inside the shaft.

The winch was winding the rope back onto the drum at a good rate. 'Any minute now…' said Sadie, and they all looked down the well, waiting for the first sign of the Doctor. The rope grew thicker on the drum as it slowly revolved and the blue line that dangled down into the shaft began to snake back and forth.

'I don't like the look of this,' said Angela after a moment.

Then they saw the end of the rope as it ascended the shaft, and something dangling from it. Martha almost choked as it came into view.

It was the Doctor's climbing harness. And it was empty. Martha grabbed the webbing harness and inspected it quickly. Through the tears stinging her eyes, she could hardly see if it was damaged or not. But it hardly mattered.

The Doctor was gone.

TWELVE

Angela looked ashen-faced at the empty harness. 'It's not possible,' she said, taking off her hat. All her usual brio had vanished, and suddenly she looked like the old woman she really was.

'Don't forget the bucket,' said Sadie. 'Something took that too.'

Angela was shocked. 'Are you trying to say something's *taken* the Doctor?'

'Let's all just stay calm,' said Martha. Out of the three of them, she was the most composed. Perhaps she was more used to this kind of thing with the Doctor, but she knew she had to stay in control. Panicking was the last thing they needed. Instinctively, she felt gripped by a desire to do the right thing, the practical thing. She had done it all her life, after all.

'But what can we do?' Angela asked. 'If he's fallen and hurt down there... Martha, it doesn't bear thinking about.'

'Wait a second. We don't know what's happened yet. We need to think.' For want of anything better to do, she tried the walkie-talkie, but it was useless.

'You said something happened to Barney Hackett, too,' Sadie said to Martha. 'Last night, here. Something terrible, you said. What was all that about?'

Martha took a deep breath. 'It must be connected, but I don't know how, right? We were talking to Barney here last night, just by the well. Yeah, he was telling us about his cat and the story of the highwayman. But then he sort of...' She trailed off, not really wanting to go on.

'Let me guess,' said Sadie. 'He had one of his funny turns.'

'Well... It was a bit more than a funny turn, actually.' Martha tried to explain what had happened, up to and including the old man's collapse into a pile of dust.

When she had finished, Angela and Sadie simply stared at her.

'I see...' Angela said slowly, as if considering in minute detail what she had just been told. But Martha could tell that her whole attitude had changed, and so had that of Sadie. They weren't making any eye contact with her any longer. They thought she was crazy.

'Look, I know it seems impossible,' Martha said, trying to sound reasonable, 'but it's all true, I swear. The Doctor knows about these things. It's not easy to explain. I wouldn't have told you if it wasn't important... but now...' She tailed off again, fingering the Doctor's climbing harness.

'So the Doctor's seen this kind of thing before, has he?' said Sadie.

'Yeah.'

'I thought he was from the council,' Angela said. She took off her old bush hat and ran her fingers through her hair. 'I don't know if I can believe you or not, Martha…'

'But…?' Martha added hopefully.

'But there's something very odd going on here,' Angela continued, 'and I'm damned if I know what it is.'

'If what you said is true,' Sadie offered, 'then that means Barney Hackett is dead.'

'Yes,' said Martha.

'Which would be a very serious thing indeed.'

'I'm not joking.'

'Why didn't you go to the police? Or tell anyone?'

'Well, d'uh!' Martha finally began to lose patience. 'Do you think I enjoyed telling you two? Just think what it would have been like telling a policeman!'

Angela pursed her lips. 'She's got a point, Sadie.'

'Are you trying to tell me you believe her?'

'She's got nothing to gain by making it up, has she?'

Martha cleared her throat. 'I am still here, you know.'

'Unlike Barney Hackett,' Sadie remarked drily.

Somewhere near the bottom of the well, the Doctor was upside down in complete darkness.

He had been dragged into the white weed like a fly into a spider's web. The more he struggled, the more deeply he became ensnared. The strange, fibrous roots weren't sticky, but they still managed to hold on to him, slowly curling tiny little shoots around his ankles and wrists until he was well and truly caught.

The web analogy wasn't one of his favourites. It implied that, at the centre of the trap, there would be a large spider. And that he was lunch. He didn't care for either notion.

Besides which, the tangle of white, fleshy roots didn't feel like something that had been constructed in the manner of a deliberate trap; it was more like something that had grown haphazardly, without any real design or purpose. The shoots had sprouted and crawled and clung to the shaft walls and eventually criss-crossed the empty space between. It was just his misfortune that he'd got tangled up. Now he was hanging upside down in the darkness, wondering what to do.

He'd already tried the sonic screwdriver. Apart from taking a few readings which had only confirmed his previous analysis that the roots were neither animal nor vegetable in origin, there was a distinct danger: every time the sonic energy waves made contact with the web, it tightened its grip. The reaction seemed involuntary, but it was there nonetheless, and after a while it began to get painful. He'd switched the screwdriver off and stowed it carefully away. Being upside down, he didn't want it falling out of his pocket.

He'd stopped struggling, but apart from that all he could do was hang. He kept thinking of Martha and the others at the top of the well. They'd be wondering what had happened to him. *He* was wondering what had happened to him.

'Bucket,' he said aloud. His outstretched hand had just touched something hard and wooden and curved, and he recognised it instantly. He couldn't see it, but he could feel it. So this was where it had ended up. Something had pulled it down here and pulled it hard. It was all but smothered in the white weed.

Not a comforting thought. But it did give him an idea – the sound of his voice had echoed around the well, and helped define his immediate surroundings.

He quickly went through all of his senses: it was something to do, anyway, and you never knew what you might pick up from an unexpected source.

Hearing – if he slowed his hearts right down and stopped breathing altogether, there was total silence; there wasn't even the noise of any insects or snails this far down, and he suspected they were instinctively staying clear of this very unnatural phenomenon. Wise move, probably.

Touch – he knew the thing holding him was warm, fibrous, not sticky. But if he moved, it seemed to grip harder. Nothing much more to be learned there.

Smell – damp, cold, and a faint, underlying odour of decay with just a hint of ginger. That was probably Tommy. There was something else, though, something he couldn't identify. Something totally alien to Earth. *Smell me something I don't know*, he thought.

Taste – he opened his mouth and stuck out his tongue, waggling it energetically in the darkness. This didn't tell him much more than his sense of smell, fortunately.

Sight – nothing. Just blackness. In fact, he could see more with his eyes shut. The Doctor was just about to start going through his extra senses, starting with his sixth sense, when something made him stop. *Wait a minute*, he thought. *Go back one.*

He opened his eyes again and this time he actually saw something. 'Ha!' he shouted. He could see! Not much, but there was something – the faintest of green glows, right below him, and indeed all around him.

The white stuff was glowing in the dark. 'Bioluminescence!' announced the Doctor happily. 'Oh, very good. I like that. Handy, too…'

He hung in the semi-darkness, looking at all the faintly glowing strands which held him there.

Now what?

'Whatever happened to Barney Hackett last night,' said Angela, 'makes very little difference to what's happened to the Doctor today.'

Martha frowned. 'How come?'

'Well, in its broadest sense, it doesn't matter a jot if Barney Hackett transformed into a monster and then turned to dust, or ran around and disappeared into thin air, or was abducted by space aliens, or simply went away to spend some time with relatives. What matters is what we know happened here today – the Doctor went down the well and hasn't come back up.' Angela had regained some of her old spirit now. 'In other words, he's stuck down there and he needs our help.'

Martha felt a surge of relief. 'You're absolutely right.'

'You mean let's just forget all about Barney Hackett,' said Sadie accusingly.

'No!' Angela waved a hand irritably. 'I mean, yes. Look, there's precious little we can do about him now – that's what I mean. But we *can* help the Doctor.'

'How, exactly?' Sadie nodded at the rope drum and winch. 'Send someone else down? Don't be ridiculous.'

'I'll go,' said Martha.

'No you won't,' Angela told her firmly. 'We're not about to lose someone else down the infernal thing. We'll call the fire brigade. They'll know what to do.' She fumbled in her pockets and found her mobile phone. Martha rather liked the idea of an 83-year-old lady having a mobile. Somehow, with Angela Hook, it wasn't a surprise.

'I've got a better idea,' Martha said. 'There's no point in calling in the emergency services yet. They'll take ages to get here and we don't really know what we're dealing with. At the very least they'll just send someone else down the well, eventually.'

'Then what do you suggest?' asked Sadie.

Martha took a deep breath. 'You're not going to like it,' she said.

THIRTEEN

The Land-Rover screeched to a halt in front of the gates and Angela sounded the horn. 'I can't believe I let you talk me into this,' she told Martha. 'I still think we could have just phoned him.'

'This sort of thing is better face to face,' Martha said. She was in the passenger seat, her fingers still digging deep into the worn upholstery. Angela's mood hadn't helped her driving. She had nearly run over a local man walking his dogs on the short trip from the well to the manor.

'Come on, come on!' yelled Angela, hitting the horn again. A series of peremptory honks came from the Land-Rover's radiator grille, but the gates remained shut.

They were electronic gates, and Martha thought ruefully that the Doctor's sonic screwdriver would have made short work of them. 'Maybe if I got out and used the intercom?' she suggested, pointing to the metal box on the pillar.

'Might work,' agreed Angela. 'But I prefer it this way.'

The horn blared again and again. Eventually the gates swung slowly open on hydraulic hinges, and Angela hit the accelerator. The Land-Rover shot forward, throwing up gravel as the heavy tyres searched for a grip on the driveway.

'Well, we're here,' Angela said as they skidded to a halt. Through the dirty windscreen they could see the wide steps and large front door of Gaskin Manor. 'That door could do with a new coat of paint,' she muttered. 'Just look at it – all peeling and what-not. Wood's probably rotten, too, I shouldn't wonder.'

Martha recognised diversionary conversation when she heard it. She rested a hand gently on Angela's arm. 'Look, I'm really grateful you came. But I can speak to him on my own, if you prefer…'

'Not a chance!' Angela pushed her bush hat down on her head, climbed out of the Land-Rover and stomped up the steps towards the front door.

Angela already had her thumb on the doorbell when Martha caught up. 'After all this he's probably out.'

'His car's still here,' Martha said, pointing at the gleaming Daimler parked further along the drive. 'And someone must have opened the gates for us.' She winced as she listened to the doorbell ringing constantly inside the house as Angela kept the button pressed. With that and the car horn, Henry Gaskin was going to be in a pretty bad mood by the time he answered the door.

Come to think of it, the door did look a bit shabby. The paintwork was badly maintained and some of the glass in the windows was cracked or the beading was in need of replacement. It seemed odd, somehow. Martha expected a big country manor like this to be in tip-top condition. The Daimler certainly was, and Gaskin himself hadn't looked like the kind of man who tolerated second best.

At last the door opened and Gaskin glared down at them. The bristling black brows and deep-set eyes already seemed familiar to Martha. 'Oh, it's you,' he said drily, as he saw Angela. He didn't sound in the least bit surprised. 'Couldn't you use the intercom like anybody else?'

'Would you have let me in?'

'No.'

'Well, then.'

Gaskin turned to Martha. 'What's going on here, if you don't mind me asking? I do have work to attend to, you know.'

Martha pulled on her most man-dazzling smile. 'Look, we're really sorry to disturb you, Mr Gaskin, but it really is important and we need your help.'

'I really am very busy,' Gaskin told her, addressing Martha with a modicum of genuine regret. 'I'm sorry.'

He began to close the door but Angela got her foot inside first. 'Not so fast, Henry!'

'It's my friend,' Martha interjected quickly, sensing her opportunity was going to vanish fast. 'He's had an accident – he's fallen down the well.'

Gaskin switched his dark eyes back to Angela for the first time. 'Is this some sort of joke?'

'Of course it isn't,' she snapped. 'What do you take me for?'

'You'd better come in.'

* * *

It was a beautiful house. Even in the present circumstances, Martha was impressed. The ceilings were high, the furniture sumptuous, the walls lined with old paintings and sculptures.

Gaskin took them into the drawing room, and the first thing that struck Martha was Jess. The Border Collie literally leapt up to greet her as she entered the room. The dog was friendly enough, just a little enthusiastic, almost pushing her over. Martha patted the Collie and gave her ears a rub and fancied she'd made an instant doggy friend. Gaskin, however, wasn't in the mood for any canine fun. He made a few abrupt noises and Jess had to settle for running around everyone's legs with her tail wagging madly.

'Get out, you daft thing,' grumbled her master, and the dog obeyed. Gaskin excused himself for a moment as he ushered Jess away with a tight, embarrassed smile and shut the door. 'Wretched dog,' he said without malice. 'Always getting under my feet.'

There was a grand piano in one corner, covered with framed photographs, presumably of the Gaskin family. Although there were a number of comfortable, expensive-looking armchairs in the room, they weren't invited to sit. Gaskin simply stood by the ornate Adam fireplace and glowered at them. 'Please be brief,' he instructed them. 'I really am pressed for time.'

'So is the Doctor,' said Angela bluntly. 'He could be injured at the bottom of the well for all we know. Or worse.'

'I said he shouldn't have gone down the well,' Gaskin

replied with a shake of his head. 'It was madness. You're all mad.'

'We don't actually know what's happened to him,' Martha said, in what she hoped was a calm and intelligent manner. 'We lowered him down and everything was going all right. But when we tried to pull him up – he wasn't on the end of the rope.'

'Are you in contact with him in any way?'

'No.'

'Then may I ask why you have come here to see me, rather than doing the obvious thing, which is to call in the emergency services?'

'The Doctor said that if anything went wrong, anything at all, I was to come and see you.'

Gaskin raised his bushy eyebrows. 'Did he, indeed? And why would he say that?'

'Well,' Martha confessed, 'I'm not sure. But I think it might be because you said something about a monster.'

'Monster?'

'Look, I know it doesn't make sense, but the Doctor's in terrible danger and I really need your help.'

Gaskin straightened up. 'Well, I'm very sorry to disappoint you, young lady, but I don't see what I can possibly do to help. I mean… *monsters*? We all know the stories, my dear, but really…'

'Stop prevaricating, Henry!' ordered Angela, her voice resounding in the room. 'We need practical help, not waffle. You've got climbing equipment, haven't you?'

'I hope you're not suggesting *I* go down the well after your foolish friend?'

'Well that would never happen, would it?' Angela demanded, nostrils flaring. 'Oh, what's the point? Martha doesn't know the sort of man you are, does she? She doesn't know that it's useless trying to rely on *you* for help.'

Gaskin opened his mouth to reply but changed his mind. Martha tensed, realising that the interview had taken an ugly turn in a personal direction which had nothing to do with saving the Doctor. Angela gave a derisive snort and turned to leave. 'Come on, Martha, we're wasting our time here. Let's go.'

And with that she marched out of the drawing room.

Martha hesitated, and then turned to Gaskin. 'I'm sorry,' she said, only to find that he was saying exactly the same thing to her.

He shrugged. It was a curiously helpless gesture for such a self-confident man. 'What can I say? Angela and I... we haven't exactly been on good terms for many years, as you can probably tell.'

Martha felt sorry for him. He looked so miserable and not a little lost; nothing like the arrogant bully she had first seen on the village green. 'It's about her husband, isn't it?'

'Roger. Fine man. A good friend – the best.' Gaskin's speech became clipped as his upper lip stiffened. He picked up a picture frame from the piano, and showed it to Martha with a heavy sigh. 'That's Roger and me, twenty years ago. I had more hair then.'

Two rugged-looking men smiled out of the photo, arms slung around each other's shoulders. They were wearing outdoor clothes and climbing gear. They looked happy and carefree, despite clearly being near retirement age.

Roger Hook had white hair, and a neat, slightly piratical beard. Gaskin looked thinner and fitter than he did now.

'Switzerland, 1987,' Gaskin explained. 'Ready for one last go at the Jungfrau. God, those were the days!'

Martha kept thinking of the Doctor, but it would have been too rude not to say something about the incident. 'Sadie Brown told me there was an accident and Roger died.'

'There is slightly more to it than that. Roger wasn't a well man. He'd been diagnosed with a heart complaint ten years before that photo was taken. He took it hard, as might be expected of a man who had led a life like his. We were in the Parachute Regiment together, you know. Saw action all over the world in our younger days.' Gaskin smiled fondly at the memories. 'Roger always said he didn't want to die in bed like an old man. He was still determined to live life to the full. He implored me to go with him on one last climbing trip. The Swiss Alps were always his favourite. I tried to talk him out of it – to think of Angela – but he wouldn't have it.'

Martha smiled sympathetically as Gaskin returned the picture to the piano. 'What happened?'

'The climb went well. We reached the summit without a problem. Glorious view – ice-white peaks all around us, nothing but unbroken blue sky above us. Roger was in his element. But on the way back down he began to experience chest pains. I suspected the worst, of course. Told him to take one of his tablets…' Gaskin took a deep breath and shivered, as if he was back there in the snow and ice. 'He didn't have his tablets with him. He said he'd forgotten them, left them at the chalet – but I suspect he had left them behind deliberately. The strange thing was I think he was almost relieved. He'd been waiting for a heart attack for years. He was just glad it happened on the way down.'

'Poor Angela,' said Martha.

'Indeed. She took it very badly, I'm afraid. She was very much in love with Roger and completely devoted to him. She was convinced I'd persuaded him to come on the trip and blamed me for his death. That's about all there is to it.'

'And she's never forgiven you?'

'Never forgiven herself, more like,' Gaskin said gruffly. 'Because she knows deep down that it was what Roger wanted, and I think she's cross with *him* – and feels guilty about feeling that way. We've hardly spoken since. That little exchange was the most we've said to one another in twenty-odd years.'

'I'm really sorry,' Martha said, without quite knowing what it was she was apologising for. She was supposed to be getting help for the Doctor. 'Look, I'd better be going…'

'I'm only sorry that I can't help you,' he said, as he followed her towards the door. 'I suggest you telephone for the police or the ambulance service at the earliest opportunity.'

He led the way out of the drawing room and Martha followed him. In the hallway was a low table in front of a mirror with a bowl of flowers and a telephone. 'You can call from here if you wish.'

'It's OK, I've got my mobile.' Martha felt totally deflated.

She kept remembering the Doctor's advice: *if anything goes wrong – go and see Gaskin.* There must have been a reason for him saying that.

Gaskin was giving her a quizzical look, seeing her hesitation. 'Is there anything else I can help you with?'

She had to say something. 'It's the well… there's something strange about it. You must know *something*, Mr Gaskin. You said yourself – there are stories about treasure and monsters.'

'Neither of which I grant the slightest credence,' said Gaskin. 'As I said, they are simply *stories* my dear.'

The Doctor slid deeper into the darkness.

Whenever he tried to move himself, the white weed gripped him more tightly. As far as he could tell it was an involuntary reflex. He'd tried talking again, calling, shouting, even low-level telepathy, but there was no response. Nothing. Just a deep, black abyss full of this pale, grasping undergrowth.

Nevertheless, he *was* moving, due to some kind of peristaltic motion. Every so often the grip of the luminous roots shifted, and he was moved further down the gullet of the well. He only wondered what he was heading for and what would happen when he got there.

He wished he'd brought a book with him so he could have read while he waited – the dismal glow of the white weed was just about good enough.

It was getting very cold now, and he was starting to imagine things in the blackness – a glowing movement in the corner of his eye which disappeared when he looked, or the distant sound of whispering, or a thudding, alien heartbeat. He kept hearing that heartbeat, although it seemed to come and go. It was always distant, but there was a definite *thud… thud… thud…* coming from somewhere. It wasn't a regular double beat like a human's, or anything else that he recognised. It was slow and strangely irregular; it brought to mind a sick, diseased heart straining to eke out the last hours of life. Or was that just his imagination?

Whatever it was, it was getting louder. Nearer.

With a sudden, unexpected gulp of the weeds around him, the Doctor was pushed down into a dark chamber. He tumbled out of the grasp of the weeds and hit something soft.

There was just room enough to stand up, but he had to be careful because the ground underfoot kept moving. His trainers fought to keep a grip on a blubbery surface coated with slime. Gingerly he dusted his suit down, removing the last traces of any weed that had got caught on his way down here.

'Hello?' His voice echoed dully but the only reply was an empty silence. 'Anyone home?'

Then he became aware of something moving in the darkness – something slow and fluid, uncoiling in the darkness as if awakening from a deep sleep.

Then, slowly and ominously, a number of pale lights opened like eyes in the darkness. They stared balefully at the Doctor and he stared back.

The eyes watched him unblinkingly for several seconds. Then, for want of anything else to do, the Doctor tried his best and brightest smile and said, 'Hello!' again.

No response. The eyes stared. There were several, of various sizes, but the Doctor knew instinctively that they all belonged to the same creature. Just like he knew, instinctively, that behind the eyes there was not a shred of compassion or intelligence.

Just a cold, malevolent hatred.

Because now he knew what it was.

FOURTEEN

Martha found Angela quietly fuming by the Land-Rover. 'I told you coming here would be a complete waste of time,' the old lady complained bitterly. She kicked at the gravel which covered Gaskin's driveway. 'That man's got such a nerve. I hate him!'

Martha didn't say anything. It seemed safer to remain diplomatic about the whole thing.

'I suppose he was telling you all about Roger,' Angela muttered. 'His version of events at least.'

'Yes, I suppose so,' Martha conceded. 'But he can't help us with the Doctor anyway.'

'Rubbish. Of course he can.' Abruptly Angela set off on foot, walking around the outside of the manor. With an anxious glance back at the front door, Martha hurried after her, boots crunching across the gravel. 'He's got all kinds of equipment back here,' Angela said. 'We'll just go and help ourselves.'

'We can't do that,' Martha protested, trying not to shout. 'It's trespassing!'

But then they both stopped in their tracks. At the side of the house was a series of willow trees leading to a terrace overlooking the gardens at the rear. Martha was dimly aware of a series of beautiful lawns and woodland stretching away behind the manor, but what grabbed her attention was much closer to hand.

Lying on the terrace was the body of a man.

Instinct took over and Martha ran towards him. Without touching him or turning him over, she quickly checked that he was still alive and breathing. 'Hello?'

The man groaned and turned over.

'Hell's bells,' exclaimed Angela. 'It's Nigel Carson. What the heck is he doing here?'

'He's fainted, or something,' Martha said. She made sure his airway was clear and helped him into a comfortable position. 'Nigel? Can you hear me? What's happened?'

Suddenly the French windows opened onto the terrace and a black and white blur ran out, barking madly. Jess skidded around the little group, jumping back and forth. Gaskin followed the dog out of the house, his face like thunder. 'What the devil's going on, Jess? Great Scott, what are you two doing here? I thought you'd just left!'

Martha was helping Nigel to his feet. 'We've just found this man collapsed on your patio,' she said. 'Can we take him inside?'

'What? Yes, I suppose so. Jess, stop making that damned noise!'

'Here,' said Angela, helping Martha with Nigel. 'Let me

take him.'

Jess was still barking like she'd cornered a cat, but she wasn't interested in Nigel Carson. There was something else, just under the trailing edge of the rhododendrons, that held her attention.

'Jess!' shouted Gaskin. 'Inside!'

But the dog was having none of it. Martha knelt down beside her. 'What is it? What have you found?'

Lying on the flagstone was a rock the size of a lemon. Martha picked it up while Gaskin grabbed his dog by the collar and hauled her back.

'What's this?' Martha wondered, looking at the rock. It was heavy, but on closer examination it wasn't actually a rock. The surface was translucent, but scored with hundreds of tiny little whirls like fingerprints. It felt warm in her hand.

'Martha!' called Angela. 'You'd better come and see this.'

She ran back into the conservatory, where Angela had sat Nigel Carson down in a wicker chair. He looked gaunt and grey, hair dishevelled and his eyes roaming wildly. Martha wondered if he was drunk, but Angela was pointing to his hands.

The palms and fingers were stained with blood.

'I don't know what he's been doing,' said Angela, 'but I'd say we've caught him red-handed.'

Martha checked his hands. It wasn't easy because they were clenching and unclenching, but she could see that the skin was peppered with tiny cuts. 'The blood's his,' she told them. She turned to Gaskin, who was still struggling with

Jess. 'Can we have some warm water and clean towels? Any kind of First Aid kit you have would be a help.'

'I'll see what I can find,' Gaskin said, pushing Jess back out into the garden and closing the doors. She continued to bark and fuss outside, but at least it was quieter. 'I don't know what's got into her,' Gaskin muttered.

Martha held up the stone. 'It's this. She doesn't like it.'

'What is it?' wondered Angela.

Nigel suddenly reared up out of his seat and grabbed the stone out of Martha's hands. 'That's mine!' he yelled. 'Give it to me!'

He sank back into the chair, hugging the thing to his chest.

'Steady on,' Angela said. 'You're not well, you know.'

Nigel appeared to be calming down. He took control of his breathing, and, still clutching the stone to his chest, sat up in the chair. It was as if he found the stone strangely comforting. 'I'm all right, I'm all right. Leave me alone.'

'Let me check you over first,' offered Martha.

'No, leave me alone. Just go.'

'But what about your hands? They're bleeding. Let me have a look, I'm a doctor – nearly.'

But when Martha reached out, Nigel twisted away from her, guarding the stone like a jealous child protecting his favourite toy.

'What is that thing?' Martha asked.

'It's mine!'

'It's OK, I don't want to take it off you. I just want to know what it is.'

Nigel reached into his trouser pocket with one hand

and took out a clean handkerchief. He quickly wrapped the stone in the handkerchief and stuffed it into his jacket pocket. 'It's none of your business.'

'I really must apologise, ladies,' said Gaskin, returning with an old tin marked with a red cross. 'My guest is clearly not feeling himself. But if you wouldn't mind, I can look after things from here. You may go. Again.'

'Your guest?' Angela frowned. 'Since when? Do you know who this is?'

'Yes. His name is Nigel Carson. He's… a personal friend of mine. Now, if you wouldn't mind…' Gaskin gestured towards the French windows, changed his mind and gestured towards an interior door, then seemed to lose his bearings entirely.

'Henry, get them out of here,' said Nigel, and it sounded like an order.

Gaskin frowned and put the First Aid tin down on a table. 'Now see here, Nigel…'

'Wait a second,' Martha interrupted, standing up. She pointed a finger at Nigel. 'This man is supposed to be digging a tunnel to the bottom of the wishing well. What's he doing here, with you?'

'Oh my goodness,' said Angela slowly. 'It's the Gaskin Tunnel, isn't it?'

'Gaskin Tunnel?' Martha repeated.

'Perhaps I'd better explain,' said Gaskin.

Duncan Goode was sweating. He'd stripped down to his vest and was in the middle of his next swing of the pickaxe, when Ben Seddon cried out:

'Wait!'

Put off his stroke, the pick twisted in Duncan's grip as it struck something hard and he hurt his wrist badly. 'Oww! What is it now?'

Ben shone his torch at the end of the tunnel, too excited to care about Duncan's reaction. 'Look! Look! I think we're actually through!'

Rubbing his sore hand, Duncan knelt down for a closer look. The pickaxe blade had penetrated the final inch of soil and struck stone. No wonder he had sprained his wrist so badly. 'It's just another lump of rock,' he said.

'No, look,' Ben insisted, pointing at a patch of mud next to the axe. He brushed impatiently at the dirt and exposed a rough, sandy surface. 'That's not just rock, Duncan! It's stone! Brick!'

'What?'

'I thought I saw it a moment ago, when you hit the last bit. Look. It's smooth, and look here… here's the edge! It is a brick!' Ben let out a whoop of delight. 'It's the well-shaft! We've dug right down to the shaft wall. This will be the treasure chamber, Dunc! This is it!'

Duncan yelled and leapt in the air, almost cracking his head on the tunnel roof. Then he thrust an arm through Ben's and they began to dance around in a little circle, skipping and shouting and laughing. 'We're rich! We're rich! We're rich beyond belief!'

After a minute they stopped and, using only their hands, scraped away the soil from the brickwork. Soon they could see the regular lines between the old stones where the shaft wall had been built. It curved away from them like a massive chimney breast.

'Here, give me your knife,' Duncan said. 'If we can get a blade between these stones we might be able to prise one out.'

Ben took out a large clasp knife from his cargo pants, and Duncan unclipped the blade and began to work. 'Once we get one brick out the others will be easy. There's some of that funny-looking weed here, too. That'll help – the bricks might have been loosened.'

'Hurry up!'

Duncan wiggled the blade into one of the cracks and then paused.

'What's up?' Ben asked.

'We ought to wait for Nigel.'

'Never mind him,' Ben said. 'He's probably gone back to the pub anyway. Serves him right if he can't be bothered to turn up for the climax.'

But Duncan still wasn't happy. 'I dunno, Ben. He didn't look too well when he left.'

'We can't stop now, Duncan!' Ben snapped. 'Just get the flaming brick out!'

'Wait. This was all Nigel's idea, remember,' Duncan insisted. 'We wouldn't even be here if it wasn't for him. We said we'd fetch him when we got through. He should be here with us to share it.'

Ben stared at him. 'Listen, Duncan. I'll tell you something: last night, in the pub, Nigel was talking to me while you were at the bar. He said he didn't trust you and wanted to cut you out of the deal.'

Duncan stared back. 'You're having me on.'

'No, I'm not, it's the truth.'

'Why didn't you say anything to me at the time?'

'There wasn't any point. Nigel was just annoyed, that's all. You know what he's like. I thought that once he'd calmed down I could convince him that you were OK and get everything back to normal.'

Duncan looked serious. 'But why didn't he trust me?'

'He thought you'd told the barmaid or someone about what we were doing. And he didn't like the way you were chatting up that girl, either. He thought you were going to compromise the operation somehow.'

Duncan sat down heavily on the ground, stunned. 'I don't believe it. I've been in on this right from the start, Ben, just like you. We went right through university with each other. Best of mates! I mean, Nigel may have found the Gaskin Tunnel but we've done everything else together – the research, the planning… all the hard work. Everything.'

'I know.'

'I mean, he always jokes about me being the hired muscle and all that,' Duncan said quietly. 'But I thought that's all it was – a joke.'

'You know he takes all this very seriously. And, let's face it; he's become a bit obsessed with all this.'

Duncan nodded and rubbed his face with a grimy hand, leaving streaks of mud behind. 'I wonder how he is. He looked pretty rough when he left and he's been gone quite a while.'

Ben shrugged. 'I don't really know. Does it matter now?'

'Yes.' Duncan sniffed and looked at Ben. 'Because, whatever he said last night, this is still all Nigel's idea. And he should be here.'

Ben considered for a moment and then clapped a hand on Duncan's shoulder. 'You know your trouble, Dunc? You're too soft. Nigel doesn't deserve a friend like you.'

'So this is the famous Gaskin Tunnel,' said Angela. 'I honestly thought it was a myth!'

She, Martha, Nigel Carson and Henry Gaskin were all gathered around a brick archway set into a bank of earth at the rear of the manor. An old wrought-iron gate, covered in rust, had been removed to reveal a low entrance just wide enough for a person to pass through. It was concealed from the terrace by a copse of silver birch trees.

Martha touched the crumbling brickwork, pulling absently at the moss clinging to the mortar. She could see a series of stone steps leading down into the darkness.

'They started building it in 1902,' Gaskin told them. 'My ancestors, that is. Great-grandfather Rupert Gaskin, to be exact. He'd grown up here with the story of the highwayman's treasure lost at the bottom of the old well in the village. Decided he should try and get hold of it one summer. Bit of a lark, I suppose.'

'Digging a tunnel like this is more than a lark,' said Martha. 'Why didn't he just go down the well?'

'Two very good reasons: firstly, the well was in a state of disrepair even then, and it would have been a difficult and hazardous operation. Secondly, and most importantly, Rupert owed quite a lot of money – gambling debts mostly.

He was desperate for capital.'

'So he went on a treasure hunt?' Martha sounded sceptical.

'The idea of digging a secret tunnel down to the bottom of the well and making off with the treasure must have been quite exciting.'

'Well, quite,' Angela said. 'A lot of hard work, though – not the sort of thing the Gaskin family would have entered into lightly, I'd have thought.'

'Oh, they didn't do the actual digging. They hired labourers. Ex-miners, in fact. The tunnel was properly constructed. They got quite a way, too, by all accounts, before it was abandoned.'

'Why was it abandoned?' asked Martha.

'Rupert died. Influenza, I believe. Tragic business. The idea was shelved anyway when a distant relative passed away at around the same time and the Gaskins inherited another small fortune, saving them from financial disaster. Suddenly the impetus to carry on with the tunnelling wasn't there any more and the whole project was forgotten about. The tunnel was left to rot.'

'How far does it go?'

'I've really no idea.'

'Haven't you been down there yourself?'

'Good heavens, no.' Gaskin looked distinctly uncomfortable now. 'I'm not all that good with enclosed spaces. Touch of claustrophobia, in fact. But you could ask Nigel. He's been down there.'

Nigel Carson was leaning awkwardly against the side of the tunnel, his face still pale and one hand stuffed into his jacket pocket. 'The original tunnel extends nearly 700 metres, right under the manor. It practically reaches the base of the well-shaft according to Ben Seddon's calculations. Close enough for us to be able to complete the project, anyway. It's taken a little while and a lot of sweat on their behalf but we're nearly there.'

'You believe this treasure actually exists?' asked Martha.

'Yes.'

'How come?'

'Gaskin Manor was used as a convalescent home for wounded soldiers during the Second World War. My own grandfather was interned here in 1943. He never went back into battle, but while he stayed here he had the run of the place. He found out all about the Gaskin Tunnel, the well treasure, everything. He handed the plans down to me when he died. I enlisted the help of two friends from university – Ben Seddon does the logistics and Duncan Goode does the digging.'

'And you need the money, do you?'

Nigel shrugged. 'I need a lot of things.'

'And what about you?' Angela directed this question at Gaskin.

'A place like this costs an awful lot to run,' he said quietly. 'Every little helps.'

'Huh! And you were always so dismissive of any stories about the treasure! No wonder you didn't like us trying to renovate the well. Probably thought we'd rumble your little treasure hunt. And we have.'

'It's all a bit academic now, anyway,' said Nigel, checking

his wristwatch. 'Ben and Duncan should be almost through to the bottom of the well by now.'

Martha clicked her fingers. 'Perfect! I'm going down there.'

She headed for the tunnel but Angela and Gaskin immediately protested. 'Hold on a moment! You can't go down there!'

Martha paused. 'Of course I can. It's the best way to reach the Doctor. If he's at the bottom of the well then I'll find him.'

'It's a bit of a long shot, isn't it?'

'It's all I've got.'

'I'd strongly advise that you don't go down there at all,' said Nigel.

'Don't worry,' Martha told him, 'I'm not interested in your stupid treasure. I only want the Doctor.'

'I'm not talking about the treasure. It could be dangerous, that's all.'

Martha gave him a cool look. 'Duncan Goode and Ben Seddon are down there – what can go wrong?'

And then she turned and started down the steps.

'Shouldn't you go with her?' Angela said to Nigel.

'Shouldn't you? She's your friend.'

'It's your tunnel!'

'Actually, it's Gaskin's.'

Gaskin coughed. 'I can't possibly go. I've already told you – I can't stand enclosed spaces. I'm an outdoors person.'

With a curse Angela turned and looked back into the mouth of the tunnel. But Martha had already gone.

* * *

'Hey, look at this,' Ben said quietly. He was examining the brickwork on the well-shaft more closely.

'What is it?'

'There's more of that weed stuff here.' Ben pointed to some thin roots growing through the cracks between the bricks. They had spread across the wall, and were embedded in the soil. 'It's all around here.'

'Perhaps it's the remains of a dead tree or something,' Duncan suggested.

'I still don't like the look of them,' Ben admitted. 'If you watch closely, it's like they're sort of… creeping.'

But something else had caught Duncan's eye. He moved back to the skeleton in the corner and knelt down. 'That stuff's all over the place, now you mention it,' he remarked. 'I didn't notice it before, but it's here too, all around Joe Bones.'

'It must have been there all along.'

Duncan shrugged. 'Maybe.' He reached out and pulled at some of the strands. Then he made a face. 'It feels really odd. Like it's warm. Touch it.'

'No thanks.'

'Wait a sec. Switch the torch off a minute.'

'Why?'

'Just switch it off – and the other lamp.'

Ben sighed and switched off the lights. Immediately the tunnel went dark – but not so dark that they couldn't see each other. Ben could clearly make out Duncan, squatting down by the skeleton, lit by a faint green glow.

'It's luminous,' Ben realised. 'The weed glows in the dark!'

'You mean it glows in the dark while it grows in the dark,' smiled Duncan. He peered down at Joe Bones. The thin web of glowing strands picked out the man's skull in ghostly detail. 'Now that's scary,' he whispered to himself.

And then froze as the skull turned slowly to look at him.

Duncan felt his heart miss several beats, and then, just as he opened his mouth to call out to Ben, the skeleton's outstretched hand whipped up and grabbed him by the throat.

FIFTEEN

The early part of the tunnel was in good repair, the walls bricked and the floor cut into a series of steps. The light from outside made it easy for Martha to see where she was going at first, but the further she went, the more the shadows deepened, and soon the entrance arch was no more than a distant white spot behind her. For a moment she hesitated, wondering if she should go back for a torch after all, but then decided against it. She had no more time to lose now.

Her eyes gradually got used to the dark but she had to move more slowly, feeling her way down each step. She didn't particularly want to touch the moss-covered walls, so she folded her arms and tried to make sure she didn't stumble.

It grew very cold and damp. The rich, peaty smell of earth was all around her now and guessed that this part of the tunnel didn't have brick-lined walls. She could hear her own breathing very loudly in the confined space. *Keep calm*, she told herself. *Just carry on. Duncan and Ben are at the end of the tunnel.*

She began to see a faint light ahead of her. Spurred on by this, she sensed the tunnel was levelling out, but there was less headroom and she had to duck under the heavy wooden support joists that were just becoming visible in the gloom. The ground was getting noticeably rougher. She guessed she had reached the newest section of the tunnel because soon there were plenty of loose earth and stones underfoot and she had to be careful not to trip or twist an ankle.

With a surge of relief she realised that Duncan and Ben must be just ahead, where the light was coming from. Then she frowned, hearing the sounds of some kind of commotion.

'Duncan?' she called. 'Ben? Is that you?'

With a choked gasp of pure horror, Duncan felt the cold fingers grip his throat. Before he could pull away, the skeleton's other hand joined the first and Duncan was completely unable to breathe.

Ben saw what was happening from the far side of the tunnel. As Duncan fell backwards, dragging the cadaver with him, Ben suddenly felt galvanised into action. He dived towards his friend and tried to drag the skeleton off him. Duncan's face was twisted into a mask of fear and pain as the dead hands remained fastened on his windpipe.

Ben, whimpering with fear but compelled to help, grabbed hold of the bony forearms. For a few seconds the three figures struggled in the middle of the tunnel. The skeleton's grip was impossibly strong, and Duncan's face was turning an ugly colour in the lamplight. The veins bulged on his forehead as he fought for breath.

Ben couldn't even begin to think about what was happening, but suddenly he knew things were turning from very bad to much, much worse.

A spark of green energy leapt from the skull's open jaws towards Duncan. For a moment, he was illuminated in the strange, crackling glow. And then he let out a long, awful groan from somewhere deep inside him.

The sound was so unnatural, so inhuman, that Ben automatically let go. The skeleton gave one last convulsive rattle and then seemed to disintegrate, collapsing into a pile of dust and bones. The skull landed with a hollow thud and rolled to a stop by his feet, grinning sightlessly up at him.

But Duncan was changing. He was standing in the middle of the tunnel, hands still grasping at his own throat as he fought for breath. Even without the skeleton throttling him, he was suffocating. His lips pulled back in a terrible grimace, revealing long, sharpened grey fangs. His eyes bulged from his head, shot with blood, brimming with fear.

Gradually Duncan's clawed fingers pulled away from his neck. The skin beneath was webbed with thick, pulsing grey veins which seemed to move beneath the flesh like living things.

'Duncan…' groaned Ben, backing away until he met the tunnel wall. 'What… what's happened?'

Duncan turned to look at him, and Ben could see nothing of his friend in the cold and inhuman gaze.

'Dunc…?'

Silently, inexorably, the thing that had been Duncan moved towards Ben, hands outstretched.

Martha heard the scream first and ran towards it. That was a reflex now. Before the scream had even finished, Martha reached the end of tunnel and found Duncan Goode strangling Ben Seddon.

Although it wasn't Duncan. Not really. The thing that held Ben by the throat was wearing Duncan's clothes, and bore a superficial resemblance to the young Welshman, but that was as far as it went. Martha glimpsed the distorted features, the writhing veins beneath the grey flesh, but then realised that she was actually witnessing a murder.

Green energy crackled out of Duncan's open mouth, spreading over Ben's face and neck, and the skin beneath started to twist and blacken. Martha watched in horror as Ben's flesh seemed to break apart and then, with a final shriek of pain and terror, he crumbled into dust.

For a second, there was complete silence in the tunnel as the remains fell from Duncan's fingers like flakes of burning paper.

Then Duncan turned to look at Martha.

'Duncan?' Martha croaked, trying to find her voice. Nervously she began to back away, because there was no sign of recognition in Duncan's inflamed eyes. No sign of anything human at all.

* * *

At the tunnel entrance, Nigel Carson swayed as if he was about to faint. Gaskin caught him by the arms and held him upright. 'You'd better rest here for a minute,' he said, steering him to a low wall.

Nigel sat down heavily. He looked awful; his skin was almost white and he had dark rings under his eyes.

'What's the matter with him?' demanded Angela.

'I've no idea.' Gaskin patted him gently on the shoulder. 'We should get him back to the house. He looks like he could do with a stiff drink.'

'But what about Martha? What about Ben Seddon and Duncan Goode?' Angela ran a hand though her tangled white hair in consternation. 'What about the Doctor?'

'I don't know!'

'But you must know something! Carson's been working here – with your cooperation!'

'As far as I was concerned, Nigel Carson was finishing the tunnel begun by my great-grandfather.'

'Digging for gold.'

Gaskin seemed uncomfortable. 'I'm not sure.'

'What do you mean?' Angela gave a sudden hiss of annoyance. 'Oh, I haven't got time for this! You take Carson back to the house. I'm going to check on Martha.'

'Angela!' barked Gaskin. 'Don't be silly—'

But, like Martha Jones before her, Angela had already disappeared into the shadows of the tunnel entrance.

Duncan appeared to be in some pain, which wasn't all that surprising. He had sprouted angular spikes from his arms and shoulders, and every vein in his body seemed to be bulging up beneath his skin. But it did mean that his responses were slow.

Martha ducked past one outstretched claw, and he simply wasn't quick enough to catch her. She heard the jagged talons swish through the air behind her back as she rolled across the tunnel floor and sprang to her feet. Duncan whirled round with a snarl and advanced again, but Martha had gained a few extra metres and ran for her life.

Which turned out to be a bit of a mistake. With a sob of frustration, she realised she was heading deeper into the tunnel. Three more strides took her to the wall of earth that represented the end of the line. Now Duncan was behind her, blocking her way to the exit. She was trapped.

She turned her back to the wall to face him. The veins were white beneath his flesh, pushing up so hard that it didn't surprise Martha when they started to burst through the skin. She'd studied anatomy as part of her medical training and she knew that whatever was inside Duncan was no longer any human system of veins or arteries. They looked like some sort of wild, pallid root growth surging from his body.

They were exactly like the white weeds growing all around the soil and tunnel wall behind her.

Weeds that moved, creeping and undulating beneath her fingers as she pressed herself up against the wall. They grew around her hands and arms, holding her fast, keeping her in place as Duncan approached.

It didn't matter how slow he was now. Martha couldn't move. All she could do was watch, eyes wide open, as the shambling, spiny monster bore down on her.

SIXTEEN

Martha felt the tunnel wall shift violently behind her. With a loud scrape of granite, blocks of stone began to push out through the soil and weed. She had noticed them before, but hadn't had time to register what they represented: Ben and Duncan had reached the well. They'd finished the Gaskin Tunnel.

And now something was pushing the bricks out from the inside of the well; the white weed thrashed like a nest of snakes as the stones fell through in a shower of earth and dust, and Martha opened her mouth to scream as a grimy hand thrust its way through the hole and grabbed her by the arm.

The hand was followed by a head, and no amount of dust could disguise the spiky hair and thin, cheery features beneath.

'Hello!' said the Doctor, clambering through the hole. He forced his way out of the gap, trailing weeds and dust.

Eventually his long legs unfolded and he fell into the tunnel, holding onto the Martha for support. He looked at her, dark eyes gleaming with joy and a wide, boyish grin on his face. 'D'you come here often?'

'Doctor!' It was a yell filled with both relief and terror. The weed was still holding her, dragging her away from him.

'Oh no you don't!' The Doctor raised a foot and kicked heartily at the grasping roots. The twisting growth seemed to withdraw slightly under the onslaught and Martha was able to pull herself free.

The Doctor grabbed her hand. 'Run!'

And immediately skidded to a halt. 'Stop!' he cried.

In front of them stood Duncan – or what had been Duncan. Taking in the long grey spines and alien weeds sprouting from all over the man's body, the Doctor winced. 'Duncan? You know,' you don't look at all well.'

The inhuman eyes bulged from their sockets like raw onions as they fixed on the Doctor.

'Maybe I can help. I am the Doctor, after all. Say "aaahh…".'

Duncan opened his fanged jaws with a roar. Inside the gaping mouth was a strange green glow, not unlike the luminescence of rotting meat.

'Ooh, that doesn't look good,' the Doctor said. 'What do you reckon, Dr Jones?'

Martha gulped. 'Well, it isn't tonsillitis.'

'A very perceptive diagnosis. I go left and you go right – *now!*'

Martha let go of his hand and dashed past Duncan on the right-hand side. She was dimly aware of the Doctor moving in the opposite direction. With a snarl of anger, Duncan missed both of them. By the time he had whirled around, the Doctor and Martha had grabbed each other's hands again and were both haring away up the tunnel.

'Ha!' cried the Doctor triumphantly. 'Badaboom!'

'What's happened to him?' yelled Martha.

'I have no idea!'

'But we've seen it before – when Barney Hackett changed...'

'Not quite. Barney Hackett collapsed and turned to dust. Duncan is still very much alive and well.' The Doctor paused and glanced back. 'Or at least he's still alive.'

They ran up the tunnel. 'Where are we?' asked the Doctor.

'Nigel Carson's tunnel. It leads right back up to Gaskin Manor. Carson and Gaskin are in this together.'

'Typical,' the Doctor complained as they ran. 'I'm only down the bottom of a well and I miss everything.'

Angela was already regretting her decision to follow Martha. She had to feel her way down the tunnel because she couldn't see a thing in the darkness. She wondered what could have possessed her to come down here on her own; she wasn't a fit young woman like Martha. She told herself that she should stop right now and turn back.

But Angela Hook had never backed down from anything.

Besides which, it was infinitely better than hanging around the mouth of the tunnel doing nothing but argue with Gaskin.

She rested against the tunnel wall for a few minutes to get her breath back. Sadie was always telling her she wasn't as young as she had been; but then, as Angela always argued, who was?

It was then that she heard the sound of a distant scream.

At least it sounded like a distant scream. The tunnel acoustics made it difficult to be sure. The long, ghastly wail had seemed to drift up out of the gloom, borne on a chill gust of air that made Angela think of empty winter graveyards.

It never occurred to Angela to retreat. Summoning all her resolve, she started down the tunnel again, heading into the darkness, towards the scream.

Seconds later she heard the sound of running feet and she was practically knocked over by Martha Jones coming the other way. Angela let out a startled yell and it was answered by a distinct cry of shock mingled with a fair bit of fear. 'Oh! Martha? Is that you, dear?'

'Angela? Is that you?' Martha's voice – frightened but relieved. 'You scared me half to death! What are you doing down here?'

'Never mind that!' said another voice – the Doctor. 'Just keep going!'

Angela felt her arm gripped and she was propelled back up the tunnel at speed. She still couldn't see a thing. 'What's going on? Doctor? Is that really you? Are you with Martha?'

'Yes, it's really me,' came the answer, 'and yes, I'm with Martha, and yes, we're all being chased by some kind of alien creature.'

'What?'

'Just run!'

But, although Angela could still do many things at 83, running wasn't one of them. 'Oh, Doctor, really, I can't. My running days are long since gone.' They halted and Angela could hear Martha panting. They really had been sprinting up the tunnel. Angela had only managed a few paces and she was beginning to wheeze herself. 'I'm only going to slow you down,' she said eventually. 'You two go on ahead and I'll catch up.'

'Don't be ridiculous,' gasped Martha.

'What bit of "we're all being chased by some kind of alien creature" didn't you understand?' asked the Doctor.

'Well, all of it, actually.'

'OK,' said the Doctor quickly. 'So it's not exactly an alien creature, more your human-alien proto-mutant life form, but you get the general idea: it's chasing us and we're running.'

'Sorry, can't help,' Angela said.

'Listen,' replied the Doctor, and then said nothing. He didn't have to. They all stood in the dark for a moment and heard the sound of something approaching from further down the tunnel making incoherent snarling noises.

'I've changed my mind,' said Angela, turning to run.

But it was hopeless. They could see the distant white speck that was daylight at the tunnel entrance but it might as well have been a mile away. Even with both the Doctor and Martha holding on to Angela, they couldn't move fast enough. The tunnel simply wasn't wide enough for them to frogmarch her at speed. Within seconds Angela had stumbled and Martha half fell on top of her.

'I'm sorry, Martha, I can't do it! I should never have come down here!'

'Come on,' Martha shouted, 'it's just a bit further!'

'We won't make it,' said the Doctor quietly. In the faint light of the tunnel entrance, Angela saw him glancing anxiously backwards. Martha looked equally fearful.

'Leave me here,' Angela said. 'You two get moving.'

'We're not leaving you,' Martha told her.

'Too late,' said the Doctor as the most hideous creature Angela had ever seen suddenly loomed out of the shadows behind them.

Gaskin lowered Nigel into a chair in the conservatory. 'There you are,' he said, patting him on the arm. 'Rest easy for a minute.'

Nigel didn't need any persuading. He seemed as weak as a kitten and had barely resisted Gaskin's suggestion that they return to the manor. Now his head lolled back in the chair and his eyes remained half closed.

Gaskin straightened up with a groan. 'Oh dear,' he said quietly. 'There was a time when I could climb mountains. Now look at me. Puffed out helping you back from the garden!'

Nigel said nothing. His head sank to one side and a string of saliva drooled from his lips.

'Yes, well,' muttered Gaskin. 'Thank you for your concern.'

He wondered what to do next and decided that a drink was needed. He fetched a bottle of brandy and poured a stiff measure into two glasses. He put one on the little table by Nigel's chair and raised the other towards the prone figure in salute. 'I hope you know what you're doing, Carson, old boy. Cheers, anyway.'

At that moment Jess came into the conservatory and sat down by her master. 'Hello, girl,' said Gaskin, rubbing her ears affectionately. 'At least you're pleased to see me…'

Jess looked over at Nigel, her ears suddenly upright. A low growl sounded deep inside her, something Gaskin didn't hear very often. 'What's up, Jess?'

The dog lowered her head flat to the ground and whined.

'Something's got you all bothered, hasn't it?' Gaskin bent down and patted her flank. 'What is it? You know Mr Carson, don't you? What's the trouble, Jess?'

The dog refused to explain, so Gaskin stood up and poured himself another brandy. He looked thoughtfully at Nigel Carson while he drank it and then said, 'Nigel? Nigel, can you hear me?'

Nigel didn't stir. 'He really is out for the count,' said Gaskin thoughtfully. He put down his brandy glass and then, very carefully, felt in Nigel's jacket pocket. He found the object easily enough, a rock the size of a cricket ball wrapped in a handkerchief. He put it on the table and unwrapped it. Jess got to her feet with a warning snarl.

'It's all right, Jess. I'm only having a little look.'

The stone looked harmless enough, although a bit unusual. On closer examination it didn't really feel like a rock, or a fossil, or indeed anything at all that Gaskin could liken it to. It wasn't artificially made, but then it didn't seem altogether natural either. It looked organic, smooth like an egg, but heavy.

Jess growled, and then gave a nervous, unhappy bark before backing away from the thing, ears flat to her head and her tail swishing low.

'You don't like it much, do you, girl?' Gaskin said with a faint smile. He looked back the object. 'And neither do I.'

There was something very peculiar about the stone. Gaskin couldn't find the exact words to describe it, but the one that kept coming to mind was *alien.* He truly felt as though he was holding something in his hand that came from entirely another world.

But that wasn't all. Because while he stared at the stone, Gaskin had the distinct impression that *it knew he was watching*.

It was moving on two legs but it was scarcely human. Jagged spines had erupted from Duncan's head and shoulders, and his face had distorted into some kind of bony carapace with glistening, black eyes. But worst of all was the writhing mass of weed which covered his exposed skin and stretched out to grope at the tunnel walls like the antennae of a giant cockroach. Bizarrely, the creature still wore Duncan's jeans and T-shirt.

The Doctor took out his sonic screwdriver but Martha put a hand on his arm. 'Wait!'

The monster jerked to a halt, as if unsure why its prey had simply stopped.

'Duncan!' Martha pleaded, trying to keep her voice low and calm. 'It's me! Martha! Do you remember me,

Duncan? From the pub – y'know, the Drinking Hole? You said I should never judge a banana by its skin…'

The creature's skull-like head dipped towards her until they were both at eye level. Martha tried to look deep into the blood-red eyes without flinching, hoping to see some tiny spark of the man she had chatted to last night.

But there was nothing. The angular jaws widened and a green glow emerged from the alien gullet. For a moment Martha's face was lit by the putrid light and then the Doctor dragged her away. 'Sorry to interrupt,' he said, 'but we really should be leaving.'

It was going to attack.

The Doctor grabbed hold of Angela by the collar of her camouflage jacket and heaved. The creature's twisted fingers grasped thin air as she was hauled out of the way. It roared furiously, drooling black spittle, surging up the tunnel after them, filling the narrow space with its writhing veins.

'We're not going to make it,' gasped Angela, falling again.

'We've got to try!' Martha shouted.

The Doctor pushed both of them ahead of him and then turned to face the snarling beast. There was no hint of reason or intelligence now, just an insane anger.

Grim-faced, the Doctor pointed his sonic screwdriver straight up at the ceiling. It gave a shrill whine, quickly building to an ultrasonic squeal. There was a noise like a crack of thunder reverberating down the tunnel and a shower of dust dropped from the roof onto the creature's shoulders.

'Oh that's a big help,' said Angela, unimpressed.

But then a huge section of the roof caved in with an ear-shattering roar, and Duncan disappeared under an avalanche of collapsing soil and rock. The Doctor pushed Martha and Angela away as the tunnel was filled with dust and noise. Gradually the falling debris ended in a shower of loose earth and there was no longer any sign of the creature.

'How... how did you do that?' asked Angela.

'Sonic resonance,' replied the Doctor, helping her towards the light of the tunnel entrance. 'Found a weak spot in the roof, hit the correct frequency and – hey presto.'

'You nearly buried us too,' said Martha, coughing drily. 'What about Duncan?'

'I don't know,' the Doctor admitted. 'I can't see him. But at least he won't follow us now.'

There was a dull rumble over their heads and an ominous trickle of loose earth.

'Uh oh,' said Martha as the whole tunnel began to shake. Dust and lumps of earth were pouring from the ceiling, and then the wooden cross-beams supporting the tunnel roof began to sag, splitting apart with sudden, fierce cracks.

'Run!' yelled the Doctor. But they didn't get far. The tunnel was suddenly filled with falling earth and everything went black.

SEVENTEEN

Jess was still making a fuss. At first Gaskin thought she was upset about the stone, so he wrapped it up again in a tea towel and, after a moment's consideration, put it in a drawer in the kitchen.

Nigel Carson remained spark out in the conservatory, but Jess still wasn't happy.

'Be quiet, there's a good girl,' Gaskin said. But the dog was having none of it. 'What's got into you?'

The Collie ran across to the conservatory doors and whimpered.

'Oh, you want to go out, do you?'

Jess gave a peremptory 'Wuff!'

And it was at that moment that Gaskin suddenly had the strangest feeling – like a chasm of anxiety opening up inside his guts as he remembered Angela disappearing into the tunnel alone. Jess barked urgently again and this time Gaskin knew exactly what to do.

He opened the door and the dog shot out into the garden. Gaskin hurried after her.

At the tunnel entrance, Jess stood and barked loudly again. Gaskin peered inside but it was too dark to see anything. One thing was for sure, however: Angela hadn't yet returned, and nor had Martha Jones.

Gaskin knew he should go into the tunnel to look for them, but he couldn't bear the thought of such a horribly confined space. He loved the wide-open spaces, the outdoors, craggy mountains under wide blue skies. The idea of going into that narrow patch of darkness made him feel physically ill.

Jess looked up at him with her big brown eyes, asking the impossible. 'I can't go in there,' Gaskin told her plaintively. 'You know I can't.'

Jess whined and went into the tunnel alone.

'Oh, all right,' muttered Gaskin crossly.

He followed her inside. It was all right for the first few yards because of the light from outside, but it quickly grew dark and the smell of earth was overwhelming. Gaskin felt his old heart begin to race. Summoning the courage that had served him well in his days in the Parachute Regiment, he fought back the urge to turn around and followed Jess further into the shadows.

It wasn't long before he met an awful sight: the way ahead was completely blocked by soil and rock and a thick wooden beam lay diagonally across the tunnel.

'Great Scott! There's been a rockfall!' Gaskin forgot all about his claustrophobia as Jess barked again, loud and urgent. She must have sensed it in the house, felt a faint tremor in the earth, or perhaps heard the distant subterranean thunder. But now she'd found something in soil, something that stirred near the ground, under the fallen roof beam.

A thin, white hand.

'Angela!' Gaskin grasped the hand and pulled. The hand, cold and shaking, held on to him with an iron grip as he hauled Angela out of the earth. Loose soil poured off her camouflage jacket and hat, and, with a sob of relief, she grabbed hold of Gaskin. He pulled her upright. 'Thank God you're all right!'

'Martha… and the Doctor…' she panted. 'They're still in there!'

Jess was barking and prancing around their knees in excitement as someone else slowly emerged from under the roof beam. Covered in soil and dust, coughing and choking, Martha Jones clambered out, followed by the Doctor.

'Mr Gaskin!' said the Doctor cheerily as he stood up. In the dim light of the tunnel entrance, his face was streaked with cuts and mud. He offered a grimy hand. 'How nice to meet you again!'

They went straight back to the manor. Martha was amazed to find that the sun was already setting and there was a chill in the air as they walked across the garden. The adrenalin was fading now, leaving her nervous and exhausted.

She shivered, and the Doctor put his arm around her. 'Cheer up! We've lived to fight another day.'

But Martha kept thinking about Duncan. She'd liked him; it had been horrible to see him transformed and inhuman. She was relieved to have survived, of course, but what about him? If the transmutation hadn't killed him, then surely the rockfall must have. She wondered about it all the way back to the house.

In the conservatory, Nigel Carson was still unconscious.

'Been like that ever since I brought him back,' Gaskin told them.

'I much prefer him that way,' said Angela.

Gaskin wanted to take Angela to the A&E department at Wardley Hospital, but she was having none of it.

'I'm perfectly all right,' she insisted. 'All I need is a bath and some of that brandy.' All the same, she accepted a chair from the Doctor and sank into it with a groan. 'I'm beginning to think Sadie has a point. Perhaps I am getting too old for all this gallivanting.'

'Nonsense,' said the Doctor. 'Keeps you young – look at me!'

Martha insisted on examining the old lady. 'No bones broken, at least. You're lucky. Just minor cuts and contusions.'

'She's as tough as old boots,' said Gaskin, handing her a drink. 'Here, get this down you.'

The damage could have been worse for all of them. Most of the rockfall had been deflected by the fallen cross-beam, under which the three of them had been able to shelter. Martha and Angela were bruised and dusty, but the Doctor had a nasty graze on his forehead.

Angela's mobile phone chirped. 'Excuse me.' She opened it and then held it out at arm's length as she tried to focus on the display. 'Confounded thing – why do they make the writing so small? Oh, it's a text from Sadie asking where we've got to. It's only just come through.'

'You must have been out of signal range in the tunnel,' said Martha.

'I'd better give her a call, fill her in on what's been happening.' The old lady paused for a moment. 'Although I'm not at all sure where to begin…'

'Couldn't agree more,' said Gaskin gruffly. He turned to the Doctor. 'I think it's high time we had an explanation. I had been told you were languishing at the bottom of the village well.'

'I never stay in the same place for long,' said the Doctor, who was sitting on a stool dabbing at the blood on his forehead with a handkerchief. 'Especially if I find myself sharing it with a mindless alien predator.'

'I beg your pardon?'

'That's what I found at the bottom of your well: a particularly nasty example of extraterrestrial life called a Vurosis. Intelligent proto-molecular parasite from the Actron Pleiades star system. They usually prey on defenceless planets containing easily adaptable carbon-based life forms, such as Earth. The Vurosis arrives as a seed, germinates underground and then starts to spread and reproduce by transmutagenic alteration of the indigenous dominant animal population.' The Doctor looked at each of them in turn. 'That means you lot, by the way. Humans.'

Gaskin blinked. 'I didn't understand a word of that, let alone believe any of it.'

The Doctor shrugged. 'I wouldn't expect a fly to believe in chemical insecticides, but there we are.' He mimed using a fly spray. 'Pssh! Erk. Dead fly.'

Gaskin huffed. 'But even so! Extraterrestrials? Here in Creighton Mere? Poppycock.'

'Be quiet, Henry,' said Angela quietly. 'You didn't see it.'

'Are you trying to say you did?'

'Yes. In the tunnel. It was chasing the Doctor and Martha.' Angela sipped her brandy and shuddered. 'It was crushed when the roof collapsed.'

'Actually, that wasn't the Vurosis itself,' the Doctor said. 'That was just a human being transmutated into a proto-Vurosis hybrid.'

'A human being?'

'Duncan Goode, to be exact,' Martha said.

Angela looked horrified. 'How?'

'Telekinetic transmutagenics,' said the Doctor. He caught Angela's look and mistook it for doubt. 'Probably. Possibly. Well, all right, it's just a guess. But can you explain why else a perfectly healthy human being would suddenly transform into a proto-molecular parasite?'

Angela said that she couldn't.

'Question is – why would it do that?' pondered the Doctor aloud. His dark eyebrows knitted together in concentration. 'I mean, the Vurosis parasite is an intelligent, thinking being. Murderous and completely without any human moral compunction whatsoever, but it is intelligent. The thing I met was just… empty. The lights were on but no one was at home…'

Gaskin cleared his throat. 'This alien thingummy…' he began, almost embarrassed to mention the idea. 'Could it have anything to do with a rather odd stone?'

The Doctor pulled a face. 'Stone?'

'It's probably nothing. Forget I mentioned it.'

'Do you mean the one Nigel Carson was guarding before?' asked Martha.

'Er – yes.'

'Guarding?' repeated the Doctor.

Martha described the stone she had found in Nigel's possession when she and Angela had discovered him unconscious outside the manor.

'You can have a look at it if you like,' offered Gaskin. He led them into the kitchen and took a small bundle out of one of the drawers. He put it on the kitchen table and unwrapped it.

They all gathered around the stone. 'It belongs to Nigel Carson,' explained Gaskin.

'No it doesn't,' said the Doctor. 'It belongs to the Vurosis.'

EIGHTEEN

'We found Carson in a state of collapse,' Martha said. 'When he came around, he was behaving very oddly – and he seemed very possessive regarding this thing. Whatever it is.'

'I thought it might be some kind of alien fossil,' said Gaskin, a little self-consciously. 'A meteorite, perhaps.'

The Doctor shook his head. He had picked the object up, examined it, sniffed it, shaken it next to his ear to see if there was anything loose inside it. 'I don't know what it's made of, but it isn't rock.'

'It looks horrid,' commented Angela. 'Like something old and dead, dug up from a grave.'

'No,' said Martha. 'It looks alive to me. Sort of... grown.'

'Like an egg, you mean?'

The Doctor shook his head again. 'It's not an egg, but it's definitely organic.'

'I meant, alive like us.'

'I know what you mean,' said Gaskin. 'Almost as if it knows we're here.'

'Yeah,' said Martha. 'Like it's thinking…'

'Ah!' The Doctor leapt to his feet with a sudden cry of joy. 'Oh, yes! Yes! That's it! Martha, you are brilliant. Have I ever told you that? Brilliant!' He was suddenly full of manic energy, pacing around the room, staring at the object in his right hand while his left ran through his hair in a hundred different directions.

Martha smiled at him, incredulously. 'What have I said?'

'Don't you see? You're absolutely right – it *is* thinking! It's a *brain*!'

'A brain?' Martha looked faintly disgusted as the Doctor continued to roam the room, throwing the object from hand to hand.

'Yeah, that's right. A brain! But not just any brain, it's *the* brain – the brain of the Vurosis! I really should have spotted it sooner. Of course, that's the trouble with being a genius. Sometimes you just can't see the blindingly obvious.'

'Thanks.'

'Anyway, this little beauty has a lot to answer for.' The Doctor rolled the brain down his forearm, flicked it up into the air by straightening his arm as it reached his elbow, caught it deftly with the same hand.

'You're saying that thing belongs to the creature in the well?' asked Gaskin doubtfully.

'Well, I said the lights were on but there was no one home! This is why. Creature in the well – brain up here.'

'Pardon me,' said Angela, 'but how can the two things be separated? I mean, isn't that usually fatal?'

'Not for the Vurosis. It must be part of its life cycle. The Vurosis grows underground for years and years, spreading its roots, getting ready for the point at which it reaches full maturity – usually called the rising. But to complete the process, the brain is added – like a kind of intelligent seed, helping to germinate the main body.' He spun to face Gaskin. 'But how come Nigel Carson's got it? What would he want with a Vurosis brain?'

'I really have no idea,' said Gaskin.

'Where is he, anyway?'

'In the conservatory. Why?'

'I think it's time we asked him a few questions.'

'You'll have to wake him up first,' said Gaskin.

Nigel Carson was still slumped in the wicker chair in the corner of the conservatory.

They tried calling him, tapping him, even shaking him, but he stayed resolutely unconscious. Martha grew concerned, lifting the man's eyelids to show only the whites. 'He's in some sort of catatonic state,' she said. 'Shock?'

'Perhaps we should call a doctor,' suggested Gaskin.

'Good idea,' said the Doctor, stepping forward. He laced his fingers together and cracked his knuckles. 'Is this the patient?'

'What are you going to do?'

'Wake him up.' The Doctor spread the fingers of his right hand across Nigel's face, so that he appeared to grip the man's forehead. Then the Doctor suddenly closed his eyes and Nigel jerked into life with a startled squeak, his legs and arms shooting out straight as if someone had jabbed him with a knitting needle.

'What? What?' Nigel looked wildly about him. 'Where am I?'

'What did you do to him?' Martha asked, not entirely sure she approved.

'Just tweaked his hypothalamus,' said the Doctor casually. 'You won't find it in any medical textbooks. Not on this planet anyway.'

Nigel Carson looked up at the faces surrounding him and swallowed hard. 'Where is it?' he demanded thickly. 'Where's the stone?'

The Doctor held it up, just out of reach.

Nigel sat upright, his hand moving towards the stone, but then he hesitated. 'What's wrong with it?' he asked, looking from the stone to the Doctor and back again. 'What have you done to it?'

'Nothing. Why?'

Nigel swallowed hard and sank back into his chair. 'It doesn't matter.'

'Are you sure?'

Nigel looked hard at the stone and then pinched the bridge of his nose, screwing up his eyes. Martha thought he was about to burst into tears. But, in a very small voice, he simply said, 'I can't hear it any more. It's not speaking to me.'

The Doctor knelt down so that he was level with Nigel and spoke very gently, as if to a small child. 'Did this stone tell you things, Nigel?'

He nodded.

'Speaking to you in your mind so that no one else could hear?'

Another nod. 'But I can't hear it any more. It's gone now…'

'I don't think he's up to an interrogation, Doctor,' said Gaskin. 'He's obviously in a state of shock. I've seen it before, during my time with the Paras. You won't get anything out of him in that condition except gobbledegook.'

'It's not gobbledegook.' The Doctor straightened up, looking thoughtful.

'I'm afraid I didn't follow any of it,' admitted Angela.

'It seems the Vurosis brain has been in direct telepathic communication with him,' explained the Doctor. 'It may even have used some form of ultra-fine telekinetic link, actually changing his neurological make-up to suit its own purposes. Guiding him, giving him instructions…'

'What for?'

'Well, what does any brain need?'

'A body,' said Martha instantly.

The Doctor clicked his fingers. 'Top marks, ten out of ten. If the brain needs anything, anything at all, it has to have a body – arms and legs and all that useful stuff. It hasn't got access to its own body, 'cos that's stuck down the well – but in the meantime Nigel Carson will do very nicely.'

'So it's been using him?'

'Exactly. Until now.' The Doctor looked serious as he turned to Gaskin. 'It's more than shock, I'm afraid. Nigel's wounded – in here.' He tapped the side of his head. 'A sudden telekinetic disconnection like that could do a lot of damage to the human mind. But why would it sever its link just like that?'

'Perhaps it doesn't need him any more,' suggested Martha.

The Doctor suddenly looked worried. 'Oh – that's a thought. And not a very nice one at that.'

'Why not?' asked Angela.

'It means it's found something better.'

'Its own body?'

'Not quite.'

Realisation came to Martha with sickening clarity. 'Duncan?'

The Doctor nodded. 'Spot on, top marks again. You'll go far at this rate, Martha Jones.'

Martha put her hand to her mouth as she remembered the way Duncan had transformed and pursued them up the tunnel. 'But it changed him – mutated him. And he killed Ben Seddon. Nigel Carson never did anything like that, did he?'

'Duncan paid the price for being too close to the Vurosis itself. He'd have been in range of the transmutagenic field. Unlucky.'

Martha bit her lip. It was more than unlucky.

'How did Ben Seddon die?' the Doctor asked her.

Martha took a deep breath, gathering her thoughts. 'It was exactly like Barney Hackett, only faster. He just sort of crumpled into nothing.'

'So the Vurosis is learning...' The Doctor scratched his

ear thoughtfully. 'Every time it gets better at it. Tommy the cat – fell down the well, but wasn't much use. Not sophisticated enough. Barney Hackett was better, but it couldn't control the transmutation. Overcooked him until there was nothing but ashes left. Then it found Duncan, right next to it in the tunnel. But now it's learnt enough to control the change, and to control Duncan – or what was left of him. Killed Ben Seddon by *deliberately* accelerating the process, because now it's showing off – look what I can do! Hey, these humans are fun! I can make 'em jump around, change 'em, kill 'em whenever I like. It's easy!'

'But what does it actually want?' asked Gaskin.

'Isn't it obvious? The brain needs to be reunited with its body. It's using whatever it can to achieve exactly that – first Nigel, and now Duncan…'

'But Duncan was buried in the tunnel.'

'It won't give up that easily.'

Gaskin stiffened. 'Are you saying we can expect more trouble, Doctor?'

'Without a doubt.'

And at that moment the doorbell rang.

NINETEEN

Martha had half expected to find an alien monster at the door, asking if it could have its brain back.

Thankfully, it was only Sadie Brown arriving with some provisions. 'It's late and I thought you could all do with something to eat,' she explained as she bustled in with a large hamper of food. 'I doubt Henry will have organised anything.'

'We have been rather busy,' said Gaskin, following her into the kitchen.

'You needn't act so grumpy, Henry,' Sadie told him. 'Angela's brought me up to speed. I know all about your tunnel, and *him*.' She nodded towards Nigel Carson, who was behind the Doctor and Martha. Nigel remained in the doorway, glowering at everyone while they all stood around getting in each other's way.

Angela said she would make a pot of tea. 'I think we could all do with one.'

The big kitchen table was soon covered with sandwiches, cakes and cartons of fruit juice, as well as a big pile of homemade scones and pastries. Sadie said that if they weren't eaten they would only go to waste.

The Doctor picked up a jar of thick-cut marmalade. 'Marmalade! Oh, it's ages since I had marmalade!'

'It's homemade,' said Sadie proudly. 'My speciality.'

'Aww, even better! And does it have really big bits of orange peel in it?'

Sadie said that it did.

'Brilliant!' The Doctor sat down and swung his trainers up onto the kitchen table, but then caught Martha's glare from the other side and immediately lowered them to the floor. 'Any toast?' he asked innocently. 'Can't have marmalade without toast.'

Nigel Carson moved into the room, and everyone fell quiet. He looked pale and weak, his eyes hollow, as he watched them all gathering around the table.

'You look like you could do with something to eat,' said Gaskin. 'Come and sit down.'

'I'm not hungry.'

Nevertheless, when Martha pulled out a chair for him, Nigel sat down. Sadie pushed a plate of scones towards him and he stared at them.

'You've had a rough time of it, lad,' Gaskin said gently.

'Don't be too sympathetic,' warned Angela. 'At least he's still alive. Look what happened to his friends.'

Nigel looked puzzled, and Martha said, 'I'm sorry, Nigel, but Ben and Duncan are dead…'

'Dead?' A look of numb shock spread across his face. 'I

don't think I ever intended that to happen.'

Angela bristled. 'You don't *think*…?'

'I'm not sure. I'm not sure about anything any more. My head feels so… muzzy.'

'Side effect of the Vurosis disconnecting itself from your subconscious,' said the Doctor, who, in the absence of any toast, was eating the marmalade straight out of the jar with his fingers.

Nigel looked at the Doctor in confusion. Such was the terrible emptiness in the man's eyes, Martha felt compelled to reach out and hold his hand. 'Why don't you tell us what happened? From the beginning?'

Nigel picked up a scone and took a small bite, chewing thoughtfully. 'I suppose it all started with my grandfather…'

'Yes, you said he stayed here in Gaskin Manor over sixty years ago, during the war.'

Nigel nodded glumly. 'He heard all the stories about the village well and its treasure. Of course, the story about the highwayman's stolen loot being dumped down the well is just that – a story. But my grandfather did find the Gaskin Tunnel. And, in the tunnel, he found something that was far more interesting than any mythical treasure.'

'The stone?' prompted the Doctor, rather indistinctly. He had the fingers of one hand in his mouth and a half-empty jar of marmalade in the other. Martha glared at him again, and he sent her an innocent 'what?' look in return.

'That's right,' Nigel said. 'As far as he was concerned it was nothing more than an unusual fossil. He was more interested in the Gaskin Tunnel and the well, but he kept the stone with all the plans and documents he had obtained.'

'You mean stolen,' interjected Gaskin.

'Whatever. The stone became a sort of good-luck talisman for him. He associated it with the treasure – kept it with him all the time, right up to when he died. He passed all the Creighton Mere stuff on to me – said I might be able to find the gold myself.

'Naturally I was interested. Immediately after the funeral I looked through all Granddad's paperwork and checked the village out. It seemed feasible. But I needed access to the Gaskin Tunnel and for that I needed Henry onboard.'

Gaskin took up the story. 'Nigel came to see me. He was very discreet. He told me about all the information he had regarding the tunnel and the treasure, and he believed that with a moderate amount of effort it could be retrieved. I certainly couldn't have attempted it on my own.'

'I suppose he offered you a share of the takings?' said Angela.

'A place like this costs a lot to run. I can't deny that the money would be useful – if there was any. I kept reminding Nigel that the story about the gold was only a story... but he seemed convinced.' Gaskin frowned, contemplating. 'Actually, "convinced" isn't the right word. He seemed driven. Almost obsessed...'

'He couldn't help it,' said the Doctor. 'If he had the stone with him it would already have been rewiring parts of his subconscious using telekinesis.'

Nigel nodded. 'It was when I came to Creighton Mere that it first started speaking to me.'

At this the Doctor put down the marmalade jar and sat forward, licking his fingers.

'You mean it actually spoke to you?' Gaskin sounded dubious. 'You never mentioned that to me at the time.'

'Well I'm not stupid! And anyway I couldn't do it all on my own. I got my two best friends from university to help. We all agreed to split the treasure equally. Everyone would be a winner.'

'And did *they* know that you were in telepathic communication with a stone?'

'Hardly.'

'They just thought you were in it for the treasure.'

'I was. Or at least I thought I was. The stone kept helping me, guiding me, urging me on…'

'The stone's influence was actually changing the way Nigel's brain worked and functioned, making sure that his priorities always coincided with those of the Vurosis,' said the Doctor. 'But the Vurosis was using your interest in the well treasure to disguise its own objective.'

'I couldn't resist it. All I knew was that I had to get to the treasure at the bottom of the well.'

'The stone's treasure – the Vurosis itself.'

Nigel looked down. 'I didn't know that at the time. But the closer I got – the more obvious it became that the treasure wasn't gold or jewels or anything else. It was something much better. Much more valuable.'

'Such as?'

Nigel shrugged. 'I'm not sure any more. It seemed very clear to me at the time. Power, I suppose. It wanted power. *I* wanted power.'

'The closer Nigel got to his target, the more the stone's own thoughts and feelings affected him,' explained the Doctor. 'At the end the two were probably indistinguishable.'

'But you must have suspected something was wrong,' insisted Martha.

Nigel frowned, uncertain. 'I suppose so. The stone did start to behave very oddly.'

'You mean more oddly than any other kind of talking stone?' muttered Gaskin.

'It became very insistent, impatient. Almost aggressive.' Nigel's hands trembled on the table. 'It started to... hurt me.'

'Deliberately?' Martha asked.

'I don't know. I don't think so. It just didn't seem to care.' he swallowed. 'How I felt didn't matter.'

'And now?'

'Nothing.' Nigel shut his eyes. 'Just nothing.'

They all found themselves looking at the stone on the table. It seemed so innocent and harmless. 'So what's it doing now?' asked Martha.

'I have no idea,' replied Nigel sadly.

'Shall we find out?' said the Doctor.

A space was quickly cleared on the kitchen table. The Doctor placed the brain carefully in the middle, put on his glasses and fished out his sonic screwdriver.

'There's a low-level field of background radiation surrounding it,' said the Doctor, scanning the brain with the screwdriver. He glanced up at Nigel. 'That's what probably killed your granddad in the end, by the way. Prolonged exposure is usually fatal.'

Everyone took a couple of steps back from the kitchen table, leaving the Doctor alone. He looked up and smiled wryly over his spectacles at them. 'It's all right… a few minutes won't do anyone any harm.'

'Perhaps it's dead,' suggested Angela hopefully.

'Nah,' said the Doctor. 'Something like this doesn't just die. It's waiting.'

'Waiting for what?' asked Martha.

The Doctor brandished his sonic screwdriver. 'Let's try asking it.'

'Is there anything that device can't do, Doctor?' asked Angela.

'Well, it can't make a decent cup of tea…'

Sadie took the hint and put the kettle on. Everyone else watched the Doctor as he made a series of adjustments to the screwdriver and then pointed it at the brain. The tip glowed and the brain was bathed in a cool blue light. No response. The screwdriver emitted a high-pitched whirr as the Doctor made further alterations to the settings and then tried again.

This time the result was spectacular.

The stone cracked open and a jagged flash of green light jumped straight out at the Doctor. He was hurled backwards, chair and all, to crash onto the kitchen floor.

'Doctor!' Martha ran to him but she was too late. The Doctor lay sprawled on his back, eyes closed, skin white. 'Doctor! Are you OK? Can you hear me?'

No response.

Martha looked back at the brain. It sat on the table, unchanged. It had sealed itself up and now it looked as dormant as ever. It showed no sign of life at all.

And neither did the Doctor.

'What's happened?' demanded Angela, looking at Nigel. 'What did it do to him?'

Nigel looked shocked. 'I've no idea!'

Sadie had knelt down by Martha and was resting her fingertips against the Doctor's throat. 'No pulse,' she said gravely. 'I think you'd better call an ambulance!'

TWENTY

They laid him out on the kitchen floor, more or less where he fell. Someone found a cushion to put under his head. His skin was bone-white and as cold as marble. He was hardly breathing.

Of course, at first they had all thought he was dead, but Martha knew that the Doctor's pulse was much slower than a human's and the best way to check it was to listen to his chest: after she had managed to quieten everyone down, she had detected the faintest beat on the right-hand side.

Sadie still wanted to send for an ambulance, but Martha had managed to dissuade her; she knew it would only complicate matters. Eventually, unsettled and strangely embarrassed, everyone else had filed out of the kitchen and left Martha alone with him.

Carefully she folded the Doctor's glasses up and put them back in his inside pocket, along with the sonic screwdriver. She straightened his collar and brushed the spiky fringe of hair away from his forehead.

Then she sat on a stool and watched him.

Gaskin sought out a quiet corner in the music room and sat down on his own. He felt exhausted, his mind in a whirl. He knew he should be doing something positive, but he couldn't for the life of him think what. The only person with any idea was the Doctor, and he was KO'd on the kitchen floor.

Jess came in, tail wagging.

'Hello there, old girl,' Gaskin said warmly. 'Tracked me down, have you?' He stroked her and she sat down by him, looking up with big, liquid brown eyes. 'Everything's a bit topsy-turvy at the moment, isn't it? It wasn't all that long ago we were wondering how to pay the bills… now look at us. Talking about space aliens and brains and tele-what-have-you. Puts things into perspective, I suppose.'

Jess gave a little whine and licked his hand affectionately.

'And who'd have thought we'd have Angela Hook here at the manor? I thought she'd given up on me a long time ago. Time was when I'd have turned to her and Roger at a time like this. He'd have known what to do, and Angela would've been right behind him.' Gaskin rubbed his dog's ears gently, allowing himself a few moments of nostalgia. 'I wish Roger was here now. I wish I hadn't let him climb that blasted mountain. And I wish Angela would forgive me for letting him.'

'That's three wishes,' said a voice from the doorway.

'You're only allowed one.'

Gaskin jumped to his feet as Angela walked in. 'How long have you been out there?'

'Long enough,' she said. She stood watching him carefully, her hands deep in the pockets of her camouflage jacket. 'This was Roger's coat,' she said.

'Yes. I remember him wearing it.'

Angela hunched her shoulders. 'Makes me feel close to him, somehow. It's silly, I know. But we all do silly things sometimes.'

'You mean like talking to a dog?' Gaskin said ruefully.

'I mean like climbing a mountain when you've got a heart condition.'

Gaskin cleared his throat. 'Yes, well. We all make mistakes.' He sighed heavily, his shoulders slumping. Then he looked up at Angela and said, softly, 'Roger insisted that I went with him, you know. I did everything I could to persuade him not to go. I told him he was being a damned fool. I told him that he wasn't being fair to you. That he was being selfish.'

Angela swallowed. 'He said he couldn't bear the thought of dying in bed. I tried to make a joke out of it. Told him to sit up all night and read a book if he was so worried about it.'

'He *was* worried about it.'

'I know. But he could be very stubborn.'

'He had to be, married to you.' Henry reached out and held her hand. 'I did everything I could to stop him, Angela. I forbade him to go. But Roger knew what he wanted in the end. He said he'd go without me if necessary. That he'd do the climb on his own if he had to. Well… I couldn't let him do that, could I? If he was going to die, then I didn't want him to die alone.'

'He didn't have to die alone.' Angela wiped an eye briskly. 'I could have been with him.'

'Not halfway up the Jungfrau you couldn't.'

'No. But you were there.'

'Yes.'

'Thank you.'

Henry didn't say anything more. He nodded briefly and then stood up. 'Right. I think it's about time we did something.'

'Where are you going?' Angela asked, following him out of the room. He strode purposefully along the hallway with Jess trotting along at his feet.

'I'm going to put a stop to this business once and for all.'

He stopped at a large mahogany cabinet and inserted a key into the lock. There was a heavy click and the door swung open. Inside were two shotguns. He selected the Webley & Scott 12-gauge and a box of cartridges.

Angela put a hand on his arm. 'Henry! Don't do anything rash! Nigel Carson's a broken man. It's not really his fault. Leave him to the police, for goodness' sake!'

'The police can't do anything here,' Gaskin said gruffly. He broke open the box and shook out a handful of cartridges. 'Besides, I'm not going to shoot Nigel Carson, I'm going to shoot that brain thing.'

He concentrated on loading the shotgun with two of the cartridges and put the rest in his jacket pocket. 'Jess, we may need a lookout,' he told the dog. 'Guard duty. Think you're up to it?'

The Collie wagged her tail eagerly as Gaskin opened the front door and let her out.

'Expecting trouble?' Angela asked.

'The Doctor thought so. Best be prepared.'

'What's going on?' Sadie asked as she met them in the hallway. She looked uncertainly at Gaskin and his shotgun.

'Henry's going to shoot the brain thing,' said Angela.

Martha stood up when they came into the kitchen, alarmed at the sight of the firearm. The Doctor still lay prostrate on the floor. He looked more like a corpse than ever.

Gaskin ignored the Doctor, stepping over him as he headed for the kitchen table.

'What are you doing?' asked Martha.

Gaskin nodded at the stone. 'I'm going to take that damned thing outside and blast it to Kingdom Come.'

'What? Are you sure?'

'Absolutely. It's caused nothing but trouble. I don't want it in my house for a moment longer.' Gaskin moved to pick it up and then, at the last second, hesitated. 'Is it safe to touch?'

'I have no idea,' Martha said. 'It was all right before. But since the Doctor did what he did…' she glanced at his unconscious form and shrugged. 'I'm not so sure.'

'Why don't you get something to pick it up with?' suggested Sadie.

'Like tongs, you mean?'

'A shovel or a dustpan would do.'

'Good idea.' Angela found a dustpan behind the door and went to hand it to Gaskin, but he was already holding the shotgun. 'Oh.'

'Here, I'll do it,' offered Sadie.

'No, no, it's all right,' Angela said. 'I can manage it.'

'Wait a minute,' Martha said, getting to her feet. 'Do you think this is the right thing to do?'

'I'm not having it here any longer,' Gaskin insisted.

'No, but… shooting it? That can't be the answer.'

'Can you think of anything else?'

Martha looked at the Doctor again. 'Well, er, no…'

'Then we get rid of it – permanently.'

'But you don't know what will happen. It may not be possible to destroy it like that.'

'No harm in trying.'

'But what if something happens? What if it opens up again like it did before?'

Gaskin shrugged. 'Let it try! This is a 12-gauge, my dear. Double-barrelled. At close range it could lop off the branch of a tree. I don't think it'll have any trouble with… with whatever that is.'

Angela moved in with the dustpan.

'I really think we should wait,' Martha said.

Angela put the pan down next to the brain, the edge just beneath it so that she could pick it up cleanly. 'I need something to push it on with, I think.'

'Here's the brush,' said Sadie, coming over.

'Just wait!' Martha said.

'Carry on,' said Gaskin firmly.

Sadie brought the brush alongside the brain. She only had to push it along the table and it would roll into the dustpan. She hesitated. 'Are you sure it's safe?'

'No!' said Martha.

'Just do it,' said Gaskin.

'*Marmalade!*' yelled the Doctor suddenly.

Everyone jumped.

'Doctor!' screeched Martha.

'Great Scott!' said Gaskin. 'I nearly gave it both barrels!'

The Doctor had sat bolt upright. His hair and eyes were both wild. 'Thick cut!' he shouted, holding a hand out towards Gaskin.

Suddenly he was on his feet taking the shotgun out of Gaskin's hands. Gaskin stared stupidly at him. The Doctor passed the gun to Martha. 'The most perfect marmalade I've ever tasted,' he announced.

Sadie smiled happily. 'Oh, thank you! I call it my Thick-Cut Tawny.'

'Loved it!'

'I know. You ate the whole jar in one go.'

'Doctor!' Martha said, relieved to see the Doctor well again but also rather irritated. She put the heavy shotgun down carefully on top of a chest of drawers. 'What happened to you?'

'Telekinetic shock,' the Doctor said, stretching as if he'd just woken from a long, relaxing sleep. 'Numbed every synapse in my head, and believe me, that's a lot of synapses.' He began running on the spot.

'Now what are you doing?'

'Getting my heart rates back to normal.' He speeded up.

'Oh yes! Now we're cooking!' He slowed to a stop and then began to touch his toes. 'One, two, three, four...'

'It's OK,' Martha assured them all. Gaskin, Angela and Sadie were all staring at the Doctor as if they had preferred it when he was lying unconscious on the kitchen floor.

'Are you sure he's all right?' asked Gaskin.

'...ten, eleven, twelve...'

'Doctor,' said Martha through gritted teeth.

He stopped where he was, bent double, his fingers touching the tips of his trainers. He looked up at her from his knees. 'What?'

'We have a situation here.'

He straightened up, looking blank. Martha felt it necessary to prompt him. 'The brain?'

'What? Oh, fine now, thanks.' He grinned brightly at her. 'How's yours?'

She closed her eyes and pointed at the kitchen table. 'I mean that one.'

'Oh! Yes! That one!' The Doctor pulled up a chair and sat down, studying the brain intently. Then he took out his sonic screwdriver and everybody tensed.

Slowly, without taking his eyes off the brain, the Doctor returned the screwdriver to his pocket. 'Perhaps not,' he said to himself. 'Been there, done that, didn't like it.'

'Listen,' began Gaskin. 'Now that you're back in the land of the living, perhaps we can get on? I still think we should take the blessed thing outside and blast it into smithereens.'

'Hear, hear,' said Angela.

'I agree,' said Sadie.

The Doctor shook his head. 'That would be the most foolish and irresponsible thing you could possibly think of doing.' He slouched back in the chair and put his hands behind his head. 'But then again, you are only human, I suppose. Total destruction is always the preferred method of dealing with a problem for you lot. Goes right back to prehistoric times, when the first caveman picked up a whopping great bone and bashed his mate on the head with it.'

'What are you blithering about, man?'

'Oh, it was the usual stuff: his mate had been fancying his girlfriend, all that kind of thing. Solution: whack 'im on the head and be done with it. Problem solved.' He looked up at the fuming Gaskin with a puzzled frown. 'Sorry – that's not what you meant, is it?'

'No, it is not.'

'Let me spell it out, then.' The Doctor pointed at the brain. 'This thing is totally alien to the Earth, and horribly dangerous. It's destructive and highly intelligent. Its one and only purpose is to propagate and kill. A single Vurosis is more than capable of spreading over this entire planet if given the opportunity. This one has been growing slowly underneath the village for hundreds of years and is now fully matured and ready to strike. All it needs is *that*.' The Doctor pointed at the stone. When he spoke again, his voice was very quiet. 'For a second back there my mind touched the mind of the Vurosis, and I can assure you that, as dangerous as that stone is now, it will be a hundred times worse if it's reunited with its host body at the bottom of the well.'

'What can we do?' asked Martha. Everyone else seemed too shocked to say anything.

The Doctor's eyebrows shot up. 'Well, you saw what it did to me when I gave it a poke with the sonic screwdriver. I'd hate to think what it would do if you started shooting at it.'

'We have to do *something*,' insisted Gaskin. 'It can't stay on my kitchen table for evermore.'

'It seems pretty inert now,' commented Martha. 'Can we move it?'

'Where to?' wondered Angela.

'An asteroid field. A star. A black hole. Anywhere,' said the Doctor, never taking his eyes off the thing. 'We've got to get it away from Earth.'

Gaskin turned to Martha. 'I'm sorry, my dear, but do you have any idea what he's talking about?'

'I'm afraid so. It may sound odd, but the Doctor knows all about this sort of thing.'

'Mr Gaskin,' said the Doctor, 'do you have something I could put it in?'

'What? Oh, yes, of course. Wait a minute.' Gaskin crossed to one of the kitchen cupboards and rummaged inside. 'Will this do?'

He handed the Doctor a plastic Tupperware box. The Doctor looked at it in dismay. 'Actually, I was thinking of something metal. Lead-lined, if possible.'

'Oh. Sorry.'

'But I'll keep this just in case I ever come across a ham sandwich threatening to take over the world.'

Somebody tittered. Angela had a hand over her mouth

and Sadie was biting her lip. Within seconds everyone was laughing.

And then Martha pointed at the brain and yelled for them to be quiet. 'Look!' she said. 'It's moving!'

They all fell silent and stared. A hundred tiny filaments were moving on the surface of the stone.

'That's disgusting,' remarked Sadie.

The brain stirred on the table as the cilia grew into waving, worm-like fingers groping for something in the air.

'What's it doing?' asked Angela.

'It's reacting to something,' said the Doctor.

'Us?'

'I doubt it.'

They all heard Jess suddenly barking, loud and clear, outside. A warning.

'Something's coming,' said the Doctor.

The barking reached a sudden, panicky crescendo and then dropped to a whimper.

Gaskin headed for the back door. 'Jess!'

The Doctor grabbed his arm. 'Don't go out there!'

'But that's my dog—'

There was a terrific noise from outside, a huge crunching sound as if a tree was being uprooted. Everybody stood still, listening.

'What is it?' whispered Angela nervously.

'I can't hear Jess any more,' said Gaskin anxiously. 'What's happened to her?'

There was a rustling noise outside as something approached the house. Sadie yelped as the kitchen window suddenly cracked as if hit by a stone. Something pushed against the pane like the branch of a tree, and when the Doctor raised the blind the window was full of white weeds crawling all over the glass like worms, probing for some kind of opening.

'Doctor!' exclaimed Martha. 'Back door!'

They all turned to see the kitchen door suddenly shake as something struck it hard. The glass panel cracked and then shattered, sending broken shards right across the kitchen. A thick arm covered in luminous white weeds followed the glass, the big hand thrusting its way inside, grabbing for the door handle.

'Get back!' roared the Doctor, grabbing Sadie and pulling her out of the way.

Sadie screamed as the large, clawed hand suddenly withdrew and something struck the door a second time, rattling it in its frame. Then, under a third impact, the door itself splintered and broke from its hinges, flying into the room with a loud crash.

And then the creature was inside – a boiling mass of writhing weed in the shape of a man, long spines standing up from its head and shoulders. There was soil and dirt all over it, but that wasn't what Martha noticed first.

What she saw first was that the monster was still wearing Duncan Goode's clothes.

TWENTY-ONE

There was pandemonium; everybody ran for the door leading out of the kitchen as the monster burst through. Weed writhed and flailed like prehensile twigs, snatching at anything within reach, tearing down cupboards and scattering crockery everywhere.

'It's after the brain!' yelled the Doctor. 'Don't let it get the brain!'

Martha was still nearest; without hesitation she scooped the stone off the kitchen table and tossed it to the Doctor. He caught it, just as the creature's heavy fist smashed through the table, splitting the top into firewood. It roared with anger and surged forward, bludgeoning the remains of the heavy table into jagged splinters as it came.

The Doctor ran out of the kitchen after the others, still clutching the stone. Gaskin was urging Angela upstairs, with Sadie and Martha following.

'Don't go upstairs!' warned the Doctor.

'We need the high ground, man!' bellowed Gaskin.

There was no time to argue. The monster crashed through the doorway into the hall, sending wood and plaster flying through the air. Its distorted bulk was too large to fit through without causing damage, but it didn't seem to care.

The Doctor gritted his teeth and raced up the stairs after the others. 'It'll trap us up here!' he told Gaskin as he reached the first landing.

'Then we'll have to barricade ourselves into one of the rooms.'

The creature wrenched the entire banister rail off the stairs and charged after them. Its clawed legs bit deep into the carpet as it swung itself up towards the first storey.

'That might not be as easy as it sounds.'

'For goodness' sake,' Angela said, 'if it wants the wretched stone that badly, give it the thing!'

The Doctor scrambled out of the way of another blow which gouged deep scratches into the stairs behind him. 'That wouldn't be a good idea, Angela!'

'Why not? It might let us go then!'

'It's going to kill us otherwise, Doctor!' added Sadie.

They mounted the next flight of stairs with the monster close behind. On the second floor, Gaskin led them down the passageway to the main bedroom at a run. 'In here!'

They all piled inside and he slammed shut the door behind them. Within a second he had turned the key in the lock.

'That won't hold it for long,' said the Doctor.

'It's all I could think of,' snapped Gaskin, desperation

making his voice ragged.

Angela sat down in a chair, panting for breath. 'That's twice I've had to run for my life today,' she gasped. 'I can't say I'm enjoying it.'

'Dammit,' spat Gaskin. 'I left the shotgun in the kitchen!' He glared at the Doctor. 'That's your fault! You took it off me!'

'We don't need a shotgun,' said the Doctor. 'We need to *think*!'

'Nevertheless,' said Angela clearly, 'I'd feel a lot better if we *did* have a shotgun!'

The stout bedroom door shook in its frame as Duncan hurled himself against it. The second attempt was so powerful that the wood split right down the middle and picture frames jumped off the wall.

'It's going to kill us,' Sadie whimpered. 'Why don't you just give it the stone like Angela said?'

'It might be the only way to save us, Doctor,' agreed Gaskin.

The Doctor looked at them all in turn. Martha could see the fear etched in their faces, knew how they must be feeling. She was terrified herself, her stomach in knots, her heart racing. And she, like everyone else, found herself looking back at the Doctor, waiting for an answer.

'If the Vurosis gets hold of the brain,' the Doctor warned them, 'there will be no way to stop it.'

'Surely there's no way of stopping it now!' Gaskin shouted.

The door bulged, cracked, split in two. A huge arm crunched through the gap, tearing away long staves of varnished wood. Weeds groped their way through the gap like a hundred thin worms, tearing more timber away, making the hole bigger.

'We can't let it have the brain!' argued the Doctor, almost pleading with them to understand. 'If it gets it, we've lost.'

'I think we've already lost,' Sadie said quietly.

The Doctor ran a hand through his hair. 'I'll think of something!'

'Doctor,' said Martha. 'Hurry!'

The Doctor suddenly ran across the bedroom, bouncing over the big double bed to land by the window. He threw back the curtains and peered out into the night.

'What's he doing now?' Angela demanded.

'We're two floors up,' the Doctor said, thinking aloud. 'Trapped.'

'Then open the window and throw the ruddy thing out,' urged Gaskin.

The Doctor ignored him. Desperately he scanned the bedroom looking for inspiration and spied another door. 'What's that?'

'En-suite bathroom,' replied Gaskin automatically.

The Doctor leapt across the bed again, his long legs hurdling the room in two strides.

'Hardly the time,' Gaskin scowled as the Doctor disappeared into the bathroom.

The bedroom door suddenly gave way as the creature forced its way through the narrow frame with a series of guttural roars. Its cluster of black eyes roved around the bedroom, searching for its prey.

To Martha's dismay, everyone else instantly pointed

towards the bathroom.

With a snarl the monster trampled its way across the room, dragging pieces of broken door and ornaments with it. It smashed the entire doorframe and part of the wall away with one enormous swipe of its arms, exposing the tiled bathroom and the Doctor standing inside.

He was holding the stone at arm's length over the toilet.

'One false move and it goes,' the Doctor said.

The creature paused, its ragged breath spraying saliva across the room. Flecks of tar-like goo specked the pristine tiles and shower door.

'I'm warning you,' the Doctor continued. 'I'm not afraid to flush.'

The monster regarded him sourly but didn't approach. It seemed to be thinking what to do next.

Everyone held their breath.

Then, quite suddenly, the white weeds growing from Duncan's flesh spread out like a nest full of snakes and coiled around Sadie, lifting her bodily off the floor. She screamed as it carried her over its head and dangled her in front of the Doctor.

The Doctor held out his free hand towards the monster, fingers spread. 'Wait! Don't! Don't do it!'

He still held the brain in his other hand over the toilet, but everyone could see that it was stalemate.

Sadie sobbed in fear as the weeds tightened around her and the creature breathed its foul stench across her face. Tears ran down her cheeks as she twisted away, looking to the Doctor.

Very slowly and distinctly the Doctor said, 'Let her go.'

The beast growled, its jaw distending and its fangs splaying out like the fingers of a hand. Tongues flapped like eels fighting in its mouth. It couldn't speak, couldn't articulate a single word, but it didn't need to. The meaning was clear. *Not until you give me what I want.*

In a small, wavering voice, Sadie said, 'Don't let him get it, Doctor…'

'I can't,' he replied grimly.

A green glow appeared in the creature's throat, welling up past its teeth, shining out towards Sadie.

Tight-lipped, the Doctor opened his hand and let the brain drop into the toilet. It landed with a heavy plop. He met the creature's gaze and then reached for the chain and pulled.

In a surreal moment, everyone listened to the sound of a toilet flushing.

Then, with an alien howl of rage, the creature leapt forward. It tossed Sadie's body aside like a rag doll. The Doctor dived to one side as the monster tore into the bathroom, smashing the toilet bowl into porcelain fragments, digging through the floor in a rending, tearing fury, pulling apart the pipe work beneath.

The creature crashed through the entire floor of the bathroom, tiles, floorboards and plumbing flying in its wake. Clouds of plaster dust obscured it from view as it literally chased the brain down through the drainpipe like a pig after a truffle.

'Dear God,' breathed Gaskin. 'Won't it ever stop?'

'Not until it gets what it wants,' said the Doctor tersely.

He helped Gaskin lift Sadie onto the bed.

Martha felt for a pulse. 'Her heart's going like an express train. It's racing – it's too fast to count.'

'Oh no. No, no, no…' The Doctor grabbed Sadie's face and turned it towards him, pushing her eyelids roughly open with his fingers. The eyes were white. 'No!' he shouted. 'No, I won't let it happen!'

As they watched, the whiteness of the eyes darkened, turning a deep grey like slate. Suddenly Sadie's entire body began to shake, veins standing out on her skin like wires. She threw back her head and screamed, green light crackling over her lips.

'She's turning!' Martha yelled. 'She's going to die like Ben!'

'No!' The Doctor snarled through clenched teeth. He aimed his sonic screwdriver at Sadie and activated it. A shrill whine filled the air and a fierce, pulsing blue light enveloped her body. Sadie continued to spasm as her human metabolism struggled to contain the alien energy. The screwdriver's noise rose to a scream and the Doctor held it with both hands, training the blue rays on the trembling woman.

Martha wanted to cover her ears, whether to block out the sonic squeal or Sadie's cries she couldn't be sure.

'What are you doing to her?' yelled Angela over the noise. She was trying to drag the Doctor away, but he refused to move, keeping the sonic screwdriver aimed steadily.

'Her molecular structure is collapsing,' the Doctor explained. 'I'm trying to stabilise it!'

The screwdriver's emissions rose in pitch until they

passed beyond human hearing. Martha guessed the Doctor could still detect it; sweat was trickling down the sides of his face as he concentrated on the work. Gradually Sadie stopped moving. Her mouth fell slack and her eyes closed.

Eventually the whine of the screwdriver dropped to a hum. Very carefully, the Doctor placed it on the bedside table, making sure it stayed trained on Sadie. A soft blue glow enveloped her as she lay on the bed, pale but peaceful. A vein fluttered in her neck as her heart rate returned to something approaching normal.

The Doctor sank back down into a nearby chair, utterly drained.

'Is she all right?' asked Angela quietly, never taking her eyes off her friend.

'She's stable,' the Doctor replied.

'What does that mean?'

'I've managed to disrupt the telekinetic field. It won't last long, but it should hold the transmutation in check for the time being.'

'How long, exactly?'

'There's no way of telling.'

'Can she be cured properly?'

'I don't know.' The Doctor ran a hand over his face. 'I just don't know.'

'At least this buys us some time, right?' said Martha.

Slowly the Doctor got to his feet. 'I don't know about that, either.'

He walked across to where Gaskin was inspecting the damage to his house. The creature that had once been Duncan Goode had torn its way through the floor of the bathroom, following the plumbing down through the next floor, and then the ground floor. From the torn edge of the bedroom carpet, they could see right down through the wreckage to the basement.

There was no sign of the creature now.

Nigel Carson stepped through the hole in the bedroom wall which led to the landing. He was white-faced and shaken, almost unable to believe what had happened.

He looked around the assembled people, saw Sadie on the bed, and said, 'I thought you ought to know – that thing has dug all the way down to the sewer. It found the stone. Now it's heading for the well.'

TWENTY-TWO

'We have to stop him,' said the Doctor, running out with Martha in tow. 'He's taking the stone to the well. The Vurosis wants its brain back.'

'But what about Sadie?' Angela called after him as they all hurried downstairs.

'We can't just leave her here!' added Gaskin.

The Doctor whirled around to face them. 'If we don't stop Duncan, *none of us* will survive the night – let alone Sadie. I've done my best for her. It'll have to do – for now.'

'Perhaps you should stay with her, just in case,' Gaskin said to Angela.

But Angela was having none of that. 'Don't talk nonsense, Henry! You heard what the Doctor said – she's stable. There's nothing we can do for her here.'

'But—'

'But nothing! Come on, you're coming with me.'

Angela grabbed him by the hand and dragged him as

quickly as she could down the shattered remains of the stairs.

'But where are we going?'

'After that creature, of course,' she said as they reached the hallway. 'I'll wait here while you get your shotgun.'

'You won't need it,' the Doctor told them.

'That's what you said the last time,' Angela said accusingly. 'And look what happened! Next chance we get, Henry can blast the wretched creature to hell. No one messes with Angela Hook and gets away with it!'

The Doctor opened his mouth to argue, but Martha interrupted him. 'Doctor! Look!'

Nigel Carson was already out of the front door and running for Gaskin's Daimler. Within seconds he had it open and the engine started.

'Trust him to scarper when things go wrong,' muttered Angela.

Gaskin came through with the shotgun and swore loudly as he watched his Daimler pulling away. 'How the devil did he get hold of my keys?'

'Does it matter?' asked Martha. The Daimler's wheels spat gravel at the front door as Nigel swung the car towards the gates.

But the gates had disappeared. In their place was a tangle of wrought iron where Duncan Goode had torn his way through. The Daimler bumped over the wreckage and purred away into the night, its rear lights coming on as Nigel found the headlamps.

A series of loud barks heralded the arrival of a rather dishevelled Border Collie.

'Jess!' cried Gaskin, dropping to one knee as the dog ran to him, licking his face in a mad display of affection. 'Good Lord, but I thought you'd bought it, old girl…'

Jess woofed and let her master ruffle the fur on her chest. She sat and panted as he straightened up and said, 'Look, Jess, I want you to stay here and guard Miss Brown, understand?'

Jess looked up at him, tongue lolling.

'Does she really understand you?' asked Angela.

'I've absolutely no idea.'

'Come on!' yelled the Doctor, who was already sprinting towards Angela's Land-Rover. 'Keys, Angela!'

'It's already open!' Martha told him as she ran for the driver's door. 'Locks don't work!'

The Doctor wrenched the passenger door open and climbed inside. Martha was already in the driver's seat.

'But you'll still need these to start it,' Angela, very much out of breath now, threw a bunch of keys to Martha through the driver's door window.

The engine was already turning over as Gaskin helped Angela up into the vehicle. 'I don't need pushing into my own Land-Rover, thank you very much!' she roared. He apologised and clambered in after her. Martha released the handbrake and swung the vehicle towards the gates while Gaskin was still hanging out of the passenger door. 'Come on, Henry!' yelled Angela, pulling him inside. 'Don't be such a slow coach!'

The two of them collapsed into the rear seats as the Land-Rover shot forwards, wheels spinning. 'Be careful with my car!' Angela told Martha. 'It's a 1966 classic, you know!'

'Hang on to your hat, Angela!' yelled Martha. 'We're going off-road!'

The Land-Rover bounced across the lawns and smashed through the remains of the gate, swerving from side to side. Jess ran after it, barking joyously at all the excitement. The Land-Rover hit the kerb outside and Martha took the bend on two wheels. On the back seat, Gaskin and Angela sprawled from one side to the other as the Land-Rover veered between the trees.

The Doctor twisted around and grinned over the seat at Angela. 'I love a drive in the country, don't you?'

Her terse reply was drowned out by the throb of the Land-Rover's old engine as Martha floored the accelerator. The vehicle shot up the rise of the hill, its headlamps searching the night for Nigel's Daimler.

'Where the hell does he think he's going?' demanded Gaskin.

'He's going after Duncan,' said Martha, teeth gritted as she concentrated on the road.

'No,' said the Doctor. 'He's going after the stone.'

'Same difference.'

The Land-Rover hurtled around a bend, struck a telegraph pole with a deafening clang and then skidded sideways before Martha regained control. She wrenched the metal gear stick into second and the vehicle raced on. The village shops and the Drinking Hole pub flashed past.

'There he is,' said the Doctor, pointing.

In the darkness they could see the Daimler's tail lights. For a second the Land-Rover's headlights lit up the cloud of exhaust like a silver ghost as the car swerved onto the village green.

Martha yanked the wheel around and the Land-Rover leapt onto the grass, churning the lawn up beneath its heavy tyres. Eventually, after digging deep, they found a grip and the Land-Rover surged after the Daimler.

The big car had already slewed to a halt and the driver's door was flung open. Nigel Carson staggered out, illuminated by the Land-Rover's headlights.

And beyond him, lit by the same lamps, was Duncan. The abominable figure was little more than a mass of tangled white weed and flailing antennae now. The long, trailing roots formed a bridal train behind it, crawling and writhing over the grass. But Nigel was hurrying after it like a groom jilted at the altar, waving his arms and shouting. 'Wait! Stop! It's me – Nigel! Stop!'

The creature that had once been his friend turned and regarded him coldly. His blood-red eyes stared at Nigel as he approached.

'Nigel! Don't go near it!' shouted the Doctor as he jumped out of the Land-Rover. 'That's no longer Duncan Goode. He won't recognise you.'

Nigel didn't even glance at the Doctor. 'I'm not talking to Duncan,' he said.

The creature still held the stone in one claw. It was glowing green now, emitting sharp crackles of energy as it neared the well.

The Doctor grabbed hold of Nigel. 'It doesn't need you any more! Forget it!'

'No!' Nigel shook him off and stepped towards the monster. 'No, I won't believe that…'

Martha caught up with the Doctor. 'What's happening?'

'The brain has to be united with the Vurosis in order to start the rising,' said the Doctor, eyes wide with fear. 'Nigel thinks it's still interested in him. He couldn't be more wrong.'

'Nigel!' Martha shouted. 'Keep back!'

But Nigel paid no attention. He walked determinedly towards the shambling creature, apparently unafraid.

By now, the people who had been in the pub had heard the commotion and were coming out to investigate. Soon there was a small crowd milling about outside, some of them still holding pint glasses. A few wandered across the village green, alarmed by the fact that a Daimler and a Land-Rover had skidded to a halt by the old wishing well.

'Wretched joy riders,' called one of the people crossly. 'Come in from the town, they have.'

'No, that's Henry Gaskin's Daimler.'

'And Angela Hook's Land-Rover! What's going on?'

The people stopped in their tracks when they saw Nigel Carson and the weed creature in the Land-Rover headlights. Someone screamed.

Gaskin stalked forward and someone else shouted, 'Blimey, he's got a gun!'

'Let me through,' said Gaskin, pushing past the Doctor and Martha. Angela hurried after him.

'No,' said the Doctor, grabbing Gaskin by the arm. 'I won't let you shoot it!'

He pulled away. 'I'm not letting that damned monster go loose, Doctor!'

Nigel Carson had nearly reached it. The creature towered over him, tendrils of milky-white weeds dangling from its hands and shoulders. As Nigel drew closer, the thing's jaws unfolded and it hissed at him. Brown saliva sprayed through the air but Nigel barely flinched. He held out his hand towards the creature. 'Please… let me have it…'

The creature hissed again, its tongues twisting in its mouth as it backed away towards the well.

The Doctor started forwards. 'Oh no…'

'Give it to me!' bellowed Nigel, and the creature retaliated by lashing out with its free arm. The claw caught Nigel on the side of the head and hurled him to the ground where he lay stunned.

'Shoot the ruddy thing!' cried someone from the pub.

Gaskin raised the shotgun to his cheek and took aim. He had the monster square in his sights and at such close range he couldn't possibly miss. But as he squeezed the trigger, the Doctor pushed the barrel skywards. The gun went off harmlessly into the night and the crowd gasped as the sound of the shot echoed around the village.

'What are you doing?' Gaskin snarled at the Doctor.

'Too many people have died because of this already,' the Doctor replied angrily. 'There's no need for any more.'

'But look at that thing!'

'Somewhere inside *that thing* is Duncan Goode,' snapped the Doctor. 'He didn't choose to be here doing this.'

'That's as maybe,' Gaskin argued. 'But doing it he is. Look.'

The creature was leaning over the well. It held the brain aloft for a moment, as if savouring the moment. The well was filled with a bright green light, shining up expectantly, hungrily, from the depths.

'If what you have told us is true, that thing's about to deliver the creature's brain,' Gaskin said. 'According to you, that could ultimately mean the death of hundreds, perhaps thousands, of people…'

'Millions, in the end,' agreed the Doctor. He watched helplessly as sparks of green energy reached up out of the well, snatching impatiently at the brain.

'Then surely one life is worth all those?' Gaskin asked, raising his shotgun again. 'It may save countless people in the long run.'

'Sorry,' said the Doctor, pushing the gun barrel down, towards the ground this time. He held it fast in a surprisingly strong grip. 'I don't work like that. No sacrifices. Not if I can help it.'

'And can you?'

The Doctor looked up at the creature as it let out a horrific cry of triumph and let go of the brain. It dropped straight down into the well amid a fierce crackle of green energy.

'Oh, not good,' said the Doctor. 'Not good at all.'

Martha and Angela joined them as the green light seemed to fade from the well until there was nothing visible except the dark hole.

The creature sank to its knees with a strange groan, as if all the fury contained within was simply draining away. The white weeds coiled madly, out of control, as if they were trying to escape.

'What's happening to it?' asked Angela.

The Doctor started forward. 'The Vurosis has got what it wants – so now it's finished with Duncan. It's letting him go...'

The creature collapsed onto the grass with an inarticulate cry. It was all the more pathetic a sight because the cry was that of a man in great pain and despair. The weeds writhed and shrank as the Doctor approached. He knelt by the creature as the weeds were sucked back into the man's body, withdrawing beneath the rippling flesh. Wounds closed over them and for a second the weeds remained visible as a web of veins pulsing beneath the skin. Then they sank away, leaving the human being behind.

Martha joined the Doctor and watched with him as Duncan's face popped and cracked back into its normal shape, the bones reforming and the skin returning to its natural hue. Dressed in the rags of his own clothes, Duncan lay shivering on the grass. His eyes were rolled up into his head and his blond hair was stuck to his head with sweat, but otherwise he appeared unharmed.

'I can't believe it,' Martha whispered. 'Will he be all right?' I mean really all right?'

'I don't know.'

The Doctor helped Duncan sit up. His eyes fluttered open and a weak smile appeared when he saw Martha. 'I told you... not to judge... the banana by its skin...'

'He's delirious,' said the Doctor. 'There could be brain damage.'

'No,' said Martha with a laugh. 'No, he's not delirious. He's asking me for a date, that's all.'

The Doctor frowned, then looked back at Duncan.

'Crikey, you don't waste any time, do you?'

By this point quite a crowd had gathered around the well. Gaskin and Angela were the closest, but behind them were all the people from the pub, now considering it safe to approach, and a number of people from the nearest houses. The commotion grew.

'What's going on?'

'Someone call the police.'

'Has someone died?'

'Is it a murder?'

'There's been an accident.'

'Wait, I'll get my camcorder.'

'Let me through, I'm a doc... oh. Well. Perhaps not...'

Gaskin turned and addressed them. 'All right, everybody, there's nothing to see here...'

'You're the one with the shotgun, mate!'

Quite a lot of people had their mobile phones out and were taking pictures. Angela had fetched a blanket from the Land-Rover and put it around Duncan's shoulders. With help from Martha, he was just about able to stand. 'How did I get here?' he asked weakly. 'I don't remember anything after the skeleton...'

'It's all right,' she told him gently. 'It's over. We'll look after you now.'

But the Doctor was shaking his head. 'No. No, no, no. It's not over.'

There was a sudden tremor beneath their feet. Everyone felt it, including those still lurking outside the pub to watch. A buzz of consternation passed through the crowd, and many of them looked down at their feet.

Angela was the first one to notice the change. 'Look at the grass!' she said.

Even in the light of the Land-Rover's headlamps they could see that something was wrong. The grass was no longer green. Every blade had darkened to an oily black colour, as if suddenly poisoned by something beneath the soil.

'Eew,' someone said. 'Look. Worms.'

Everyone looked down at their feet, where the ground was beginning to squirm. Hundreds of worms were crawling out of the earth, oozing from the soil in a sudden, horrifying exodus. A lot of the women – and some of the men – screamed and ran as the worms continued to emerge, until the entire village green was alive with a glistening, rippling carpet.

'What's happening?' Martha said, revolted and fascinated at the same time. She helped Duncan into Angela's Land-Rover and climbed up onto the footplate to avoid the crawling mass at her feet.

'They're trying to escape,' said the Doctor.

'Escape what?'

'That,' he replied, pointing at the well.

The green glow had returned, but this time it was much brighter. It shone fiercely up into the night like a search beam, casting a strange alien pallor across the clouds above. The light seemed to pulse in time to a desperate, awful heart beat unlike anything Martha had ever heard before.

And then, inside the green glow, something moved. Thin white fingers crept over the edge of the parapet, hundreds of them, creeping over the wall and down the outside of it like something boiling over in a pan.

And then, in the midst of the groping weeds, the Vurosis started to emerge from the well.

TWENTY-THREE

The green glow flickered as the creature crawled up the shaft, filling the head of the well with a profusion of brown, segmented tentacles. They rose from the shaft like a cluster of snakes searching for prey, probing at the wall, the stanchions, the broken windlass. They wrapped around the spindle like thick ropes, and then with a grinding, crunching roar, the wooden beam broke in two.

'It's... enormous,' Martha breathed, reaching out automatically and grasping the Doctor by the hand. She felt the reassuring pressure of his grip, and when she looked at him she could see his expression of awe as the monster continued to spew out of the earth.

A crusty, carbuncled head emerged from the shaft, the tentacles rooted inside it like those of a squid. Beneath the gnarled carapace was a moist, puckered mouth. It opened and closed spasmodically, revealed rings of tiny, spine-like teeth strung with mucus. At once the orifice dilated and emitted a loud, piercing hiss. Slime sprayed through the air on a gust of fetid breath.

'It's been growing down there for years, remember,' the Doctor said as they began to back away. 'It's spread out beneath the well, beneath the whole village probably.'

Martha could feel the rising panic thudding in her chest as the Vurosis oozed further out of the well like toothpaste from a tube. Around the glistening body, sharp spines were emerging like barbs, extending and then waving like antennae. The mouth was still sucking in air, hyperventilating as if the creature was building up to something. 'What's it going to do?' she asked the Doctor.

'I don't know.'

'How can we stop it?'

'I don't know.'

Martha looked at him again. His long, angular face was taut with fear, his eyes wide and anxious. The Vurosis was still climbing, a long, segmented body rising from the well-shaft trailing long, prehensile white roots. The roots began to creep down the wall and onto the grass.

By now many people were screaming and running. Angela was in the driver's seat of the Land-Rover, struggling to get it started.

Gaskin joined the Doctor and Martha and raised his shotgun. 'Don't try to stop me this time, Doctor,' he growled.

'Feel free,' the Doctor told him. 'Won't do any good.'

Gaskin put the gun to his shoulder, aimed at the monstrous thing crawling out of the well, and pulled the triggers. Both barrels discharged with a deafening crack, and a cloud of shot tore into the creature's dirt-streaked hide.

The Vurosis let out a gasping snarl, and a brown tentacle snapped down and wrenched the shotgun out of Gaskin's hands.

'Told you,' said the Doctor.

Gaskin looked at his empty hands in disbelief. 'What now?'

'Retaliation, I imagine.'

The ground trembled and, all over the village green, thin white roots emerged from the grass, forced up out of the earth like needles. They extended, stretching, wavering, and all of them seemed to be concentrated in clusters where people were still standing.

The weeds attacked whoever was nearest, suddenly attaching themselves to their flesh. One of them was Lucy, the barmaid from the Drinking Hole. She let out a blood-curdling shriek as the roots rose up and overwhelmed her. Within seconds, she was completely submerged.

The same thing was happening with other people. The Doctor ran from person to person with Martha, helping to pull them free before the weeds could get a grip, shoving them away towards the edge of the village green.

Sometimes they arrived too late, and could do nothing but stare in horror as some poor person disappeared beneath the writhing growth, their own mouths and nostrils filled with the pale weed before a single cry for help could be heard.

The white roots spurted from the ground beneath Gaskin, jerking towards his legs, but he was pulled out of the way just in time. 'Get back to the Land-Rover!' yelled the Doctor, pushing him towards the approaching vehicle. Angela was at the wheel, driving across the undulating green, crushing the flailing weed beneath the muddy wheels. She skidded to a halt, and Gaskin climbed in next to Duncan Goode. As soon as the door shut, she hit the accelerator. The Land-Rover lurched off, heading away from the well. Martha caught a glimpse of Duncan's face looking out of the back window at her.

'What about us?' asked Martha. She and the Doctor were left stranded in the middle of a mud bath heaving with Vurosis weeds. But the Doctor was already tearing off in another direction altogether, heading for someone else nearer the well.

Nigel Carson was crawling along on his hands and knees towards the Vurosis, ignoring the white tendrils that snatched at his ankles and wrists. 'No! It's me!' he cried. 'It's Nigel! I'm here!'

Martha couldn't believe what she was seeing. 'What does he think he's doing?'

'He still thinks the brain is going to talk to him again.'

'He must be crazy.'

'Desperate,' the Doctor corrected her. 'But then, so are we.'

'What?' Martha watched as the Doctor ran after Nigel. She hurried after him, guessing that it was only the fact that they had kept moving that had saved them from the weeds so far.

Nigel rose up on his knees before the Vurosis, like a supplicant at prayer. He held his hands aloft and cried out to it once more. 'Why did you leave me?' he implored. 'Why?'

All at once Martha realised he was addressing a particular part of the creature which now curled out from the well-shaft like an enormous maggot crawling out of the ground. A convoluted series of interlocking cartilage plates shifted as Nigel spoke, opening like the flowers of a petal to reveal a cluster of blood-red eyes the size of melons. Each eyeball was veined with milky lines and had a central, gleaming black pupil. They all moved independently, revolving in the flesh, some of them bulging out as if seeking a better view of the man kneeling before them.

'Can't you hear me?' Nigel wailed. 'Do you even recognise me?'

A hole opened up beneath the distending eyes with a horrible sucking noise. A green light shone from inside it, and as the hole widened Martha saw, and recognised, the stone that belonged to Nigel. It was shining with a rich, emerald light.

-nigel carson-

Nigel sat bolt upright and sobbed with relief. 'Yes! Yes! It's me!'

-you have been very useful to me-

Martha looked at the Doctor, a question on her face. He nodded grimly. 'Yes. I can hear it too.'

'Oh, please, thank you, thank you…' babbled Nigel. He edged forward on his knees, squelching through the mud. 'I thought you had forgotten me!'

-not forgotten-

'Thank goodness!'

-just ignored-

'What?' Nigel frowned in disbelief. 'What do you mean, ignored?'

-you were useful to me-

The brain glowed brighter.

-but not any more-

A blinding spark licked from the mouth of the Vurosis and connected with Nigel Carson's head. He was instantly enveloped in a cocoon of shimmering green light. He threw back his head and arms and screamed, long and hard, as his body blackened and cracked and then crumbled into glowing fragments. The light died as the mouth closed with a rasp, and the human remains were scattered in the mud like dying embers. Within moments they had faded to nothing more than bits of grey clinker and dust.

There was silence for a few seconds, and then Martha heard a slow, deliberate hand clap.

'Oh, very good,' said the Doctor. 'Instant biomutation – every cell in the body changes too fast and overloads. The energy increase has nowhere to go, so *phff*! Zap! Gone! Of course, I've seen it before. Remember Barney Hackett?'

There was a pause.

-you address me-

'Yeah, that's right.' The Doctor stalked forwards, hands in pockets. 'Vurosis, isn't it? From somewhere near Actron Pleiades?'

-you understand my origin-

'I understand quite a lot of things. Quantum physics and time travel. Black hole theory and cellular regeneration. I even understand cricket. But what I *can't* understand… is why you did that to poor Nigel.'

-he was no longer useful-

'Seems a little harsh.'

-that is irrelevant-

'Ah. I thought you'd say something like that.'

-what are you? you are not like these other things-

'I'm the Doctor.'

-you are not of this world-

'No, I'm just a guest here. A bit like you.' The Doctor pulled a face. 'Well, when I say a bit like you, of course I don't mean *anything like you*. For one thing I don't have tentacles. And for another, my brain isn't detachable. You know, that must be a pretty useful knack to have.' A frown crossed the Doctor's face. 'Then again, I can't think what for.'

-i have no interest in you-

'What? No interest at all? Surely you want an autograph.' The Doctor smiled and winked. 'They usually do.'

Martha moved a step closer to the Doctor. 'What are you doing?' she whispered.

'I've no idea. What are you doing?'

'Watching you talk yourself into an early grave. That thing could kill you like *that*.' Martha snapped her fingers.

'It could – but it hasn't. Interesting, isn't it?'

The Vurosis may have been listening to this exchange, or it may not. It was impossible to tell. For all Martha knew, it had already lost interest in the Doctor. White roots were still creeping through the mud, probing at their feet and ankles, but apparently willing to leave them alone for now. Whatever that meant Martha could not guess.

She risked a glance behind her. What she saw was like a vision from another world. The village green had disappeared. In its place was a carpet of white weed, stalks waving out of the mud like the fingers of a hundred corpses searching for a way out of the grave. Here and there were larger clumps of the strange plant-like growth, some a couple of metres high, like small, twisted trees made of bone. They were the remains of the people who had been caught on the green when the Vurosis retaliated.

Further out, right at the edge of what once had been a perfect lawn, there was movement. Thin, wire-like strands, knotted with what looked like thorns, were rising from the ground. They grew rapidly, extending up and around the area, forming a barrier around the village green like a wall of brambles. Beyond them, Martha could see Angela's Land-Rover. Soon it had all but disappeared behind a forest of thorns.

'It's cutting us off,' said the Doctor surprisingly calmly. 'An exclusion zone around the well. Why?'

'Does it matter?' Martha could hardly speak. 'It's won, hasn't it?'

'Has it? Why's it growing a big, thorny wall around us, then?'

'What do you mean?'

'It's protecting itself,' the Doctor told her quietly. 'Which means it's vulnerable.'

'How?' Martha looked back at the Vurosis. It was still oozing slowly from the well-shaft.

'I wonder…' The Doctor stepped closer to the well and then spoke loudly. 'Must be an awful tight fit in that well.

Don't tell me you're stuck!'

The Vurosis leaned down, its brain glowing fiercely in its socket.

-i will grow-

'And then what?' The Doctor pursed his lips in thought. 'No, don't tell me: you'll spread out over the whole planet, destroying everything and everyone in your path.'

-i will grow and thrive-

The Doctor turned to Martha. 'There you are, Martha. What did I tell you? The Vurosis is nothing more than a type of weed. Alien, yes. Virulent, certainly. But at the end of the day – just a weed. And it'll do exactly what all weeds do – grow, and spread, and choke the life out of everything else around them.'

'So what we need is some weedkiller?'

'Good try, but wrong. This isn't really a plant, or even an animal. There are no toxins on Earth that could harm it. Left to its own devices, it will extend its roots deeper and deeper into the ground, extending far beyond Creighton Mere, the surrounding villages, Derbyshire, the north of England... it will never stop, and nothing will stop it. As it spreads, it will reproduce more versions of itself, which in turn will spread and reproduce as well. Before long, it'll cover the whole of England, then Great Britain...'

Martha shook her head. 'No, that can't happen. Somehow they'll find a way to stop it.'

The Doctor raised an eyebrow. '"They"?'

'The authorities. The Government – the Army. They'll blast it or burn it or something.'

'Nah.' The Doctor put his hands in his pockets. 'They'll

never get it all. It'll spread too deep, too far. And if there's even a bit of it left alive, it'll find a way to grow. That's what the Vurosis does – survives, grows, spreads, kills.' Now the Doctor looked directly at her. 'If we're going to stop it, it's got to be here, now, while it's still vulnerable.'

'While it's building its protective barrier?'

'Yeah.' The Doctor turned on his heel and looked at the thorny growth. He lowered his voice. 'But what's it protecting itself from?'

'And why hasn't it zapped us into dust?'

'Ooh! Oh! That's a good question!' The Doctor's eyes widened as his brain moved up a gear. 'I wonder…' He tailed off and then slapped his forehead. 'I know!'

'What?'

'Look all around you! Look at what it's doing – growing stuff, spreading its roots, manufacturing a nice little nest for itself.' The thorns had grown much higher now, curving inwards towards the Vurosis as if forming a huge, tangled dome of brambles over the village green. 'It's been cooped up down the bottom of that well for so long, this is the first chance it's ever had to flex its muscles properly.'

'So?'

'So what does it need for all that sudden, accelerated growth?'

'Energy.'

'Top of the class, again! Which means there's no more energy left to transmutate us into oblivion. Simply put – it's leaving us alone while it concentrates on a more important task!'

Martha nodded. 'And I suppose it's leaving us alone

because we don't pose any kind of threat.'

'Martha Jones!' The Doctor gave her an admonishing look. 'Shame on you! Us? Not pose a threat to an alien weed trying to destroy all life on Earth? We can pose a threat to anything if we put our minds to it.'

'How?'

'We put our minds to it.' The Doctor tapped the side of his head energetically. 'That thing can mutate every cell in your body by telekinesis, remember. But it has to keep that mental hold if it wants to maintain the transformation. Duncan changed back to human form as soon as the Vurosis broke the telekinetic link. That's its weakness!'

'Weakness?'

The Doctor straightened up, turning to face the Vurosis and squaring his shoulders. 'Hey, you! Weed! I want a word with you.'

-do not interrupt the nesting-

'Sorry, this is important. Small matter of life and death. This planet's life and your death.'

-if you persist i will destroy you-

'What? Really?' The Doctor scoffed. 'Use your telekinetic power to warp every cell in my body into your shape? I doubt it!'

-i will destroy you-

'No way! You couldn't transmutate your way out of a paper bag!'

'Doctor...' warned Martha.

But it was too late. With a savage hiss, the Vurosis opened its circular maw and exposed the glowing brain within. Before she could do anything, Martha saw the flash of green light spitting out towards the Doctor. A yell of anguish built inside her throat as the emerald spark connected with the Doctor's forehead.

'Won't... work on me,' he gasped. His voice sounded strained and he was already being forced to his knees as the Vurosis energy bore down on him. 'My mind is stronger... than a human's,' the Doctor groaned. 'You... can't... bend... it... so... easily...'

But it could. The Doctor sagged beneath the onslaught of the green ray, his face contorted in agony. Martha knew then without any doubt that the Doctor had seriously underestimated the power of the Vurosis. His head snapped up, twisting around until his eyes stared straight into hers, full of pain and fear.

And then the change began. As she watched, almost overcome by panic and anger, Martha saw the veins in the Doctor's head and face bulge and rise up, whitening, about to break out like wires through the skin.

Martha felt herself paralysed, almost faint with fear.

The Doctor's hand stretched up towards her, the fingers already beginning to twist out of shape.

TWENTY-FOUR

Angela sat at the wheel of her Land-Rover and cursed loudly.

If Gaskin was shocked by such colourful language, he didn't show it. His attention was focused on the strange wall of brambles that had grown, like something from a fairy tale, right around the village green. The stems were wire-thin, barbed with long, vicious thorns, curving up towards the night sky over the well.

It was a surreal vision. The street lights outside the Drinking Hole cast an unearthly glow over the spiky dome, making it look like a vast, alien pustule on the face of the Earth. The brambles – or whatever they actually were – were still growing as they watched, extruding from the ground beneath their feet, bending and weaving themselves together to form an impenetrable barrier.

Villagers had gathered around the dome, although almost all of them were keeping their distance. Many were talking on mobile phones or taking pictures. Someone ran out of the pub to say that the police had been called, along with the ambulance service and the fire brigade.

'Might as well call in the Marines as well,' muttered Gaskin.

'What do you mean?'

'They won't get here in time. The Doctor and Martha are inside that thing – trapped. They could be dead already for all we know.'

Duncan leaned forward between the front seats. His face was pale and haggard, but otherwise back to normal. 'But we don't know,' he said. 'They could still be alive.'

'What can we do, though?' Gaskin asked, gesturing impatiently at the forest of thorns. 'Look at that thing! It's the perfect barrier.'

'It wants to keep us out, then,' Duncan said.

'You know,' said Angela, her eyes narrowing, 'I really don't feel like doing anything that thing wants, do you?'

'What on earth do you mean?' asked Gaskin.

'Well, as Duncan says… it clearly wants to keep us out. I don't think we should give it that satisfaction, do you?'

'I don't think there's much we can do about it.'

'Really?'

She straightened her bush hat and then turned the key in the ignition. The Land-Rover rumbled into life.

'Where are you going?' Gaskin asked.

'I'm going to see why it's so keen to keep us out.'

She put the Land-Rover into gear, turned the wheels towards the thorns and then put her foot down.

* * *

Automatically, Martha grasped the Doctor's outstretched hand.

His fingers felt hard and bony, but they grabbed hold of her hand and squeezed. It was all she needed. Somewhere inside, the Doctor was reached out to her – not just physically, but mentally. He needed her.

He needed her to *do something*.

She forced herself to look into his eyes. They were bloodshot, wide with pain, but inside them the Doctor's intelligence still burned fiercely. It wasn't the insane stare of someone driven beyond their ability to think or act. It was a look that implored her to help.

And then, in a flash, she saw it.

The Vurosis was trying to force the Doctor to change, to mutate so fast that his molecular structure ignited and blew itself into dust. Just like it had with Barney Hackett, and Ben Seddon, and Nigel Carson.

But the Doctor was resisting it.

His body was palpitating, rippling before her eyes as the cells within twisted and turned, but he was holding the damage at bay.

But now he was asking her to help. He couldn't do it alone.

She held his hand tightly in both of hers, as tightly as she could manage, and nodded. Then she looked up at the Vurosis, and the flickering green diamond of its brain.

Martha closed her eyes. She let the green glow envelop her, felt the first tendrils of power sneaking into her mind, alien and cold and malignant.

It was strong. She sensed its power and intention. She

sensed the way in which it tried to change her, to dominate her. She even felt it when her body began to change and mutate, causing her to panic and almost let go of the Doctor's hand. Her veins seemed to fill with something other than her blood, something that was as cold as ice and yet burning in its intensity. It was as if a sudden floodgate had been opened deep inside her, precipitating a massive and comprehensive transformation that she could not control.

But the Doctor's hand kept its grip on hers, and his mind was there too, somewhere, because she could sense him as well as the Vurosis.

'Concentrate, Martha! Keep holding it back!'

-you will not stop me-

Martha let out an involuntary cry, whether it was pain or fear she wasn't sure. 'I can't… It's too powerful…'

The Doctor's voice again, clear in her head: 'Yes, you can. You can halt the transformation. Reverse it! Sadie's was halted, remember. Duncan's was reversed. We *can* do it!'

The Vurosis renewed its attack and Martha felt the change sweeping through her system, literally sensed the veins beneath her skin beginning to respond to its telekinetic effort.

-you will not stop me-

'I can't do it, Doctor! It's too strong!'

'You must! Together we must!'

-YOU WILL NOT STOP ME-

The searing heat of the transmutation overtook her. Martha felt something burning deep within her, at the very core of her being, transforming everything that was human. Her eyes opened, slowly, agonisingly, and in the milky blur of her vision she saw the Doctor.

Or what had once been the Doctor.

Now there was a mass of writhing white weed surrounding his wide, brown eyes, the lips drawn back from his teeth in a feral cry.

The Land-Rover punched right through the thorn barrier, ripping the long wire-like stems apart. The thorns scratched at the vehicle, almost as if they were reacting to its intrusion and were determined to stop it. They dug deep into the metal hide of the car, forcing a series of screeching protests from the old, worn bodywork. The engine roared and the wheels clawed at the ground, churning into the white weed.

Angela kept her foot hard down on the throttle and dropped down a gear, forcing the engine into a metallic shriek. Her knuckles were bone-white on the steering wheel as the veteran Land-Rover bucked and rattled under her grip.

'Keep going!' bellowed Gaskin. 'We're getting through!'

He was holding on to the dashboard, willing the machine on. The Land-Rover reared and then surged forward, the last of the brambles scraping the dark green paint off in strips.

But it was free.

'Ha!' barked Angela gleefully. 'Take that, you blasted alien monstrosity! This isn't just Earth you're trying to invade. It's England!'

The Land-Rover slewed around as it skidded on the weed, narrowly avoiding the large, gnarled growth containing the barmaid Lucy. Angela swung the wheel and the Land-Rover turned, tipping onto two wheels before crashing back down and speeding towards the well.

It was an eerie, twilight world of pale, alien weed. It was almost like a giant snow globe containing the well and the monster squeezing itself out of it like an enormous worm.

And in front of it, lit by a halo of putrescent green light, were the Doctor and Martha.

'They're still alive!' Duncan said, pointing.

'Are you sure?' Gaskin asked as the Land-Rover came to a stop. Without thinking, he was already opening the passenger door to step outside.

Angela had climbed down from the driver's seat. 'Of course he's sure! Look!'

Martha and the Doctor were crouched in front of the Vurosis, hands clasped together. The Doctor was clearly in a bad way, but he still looked up at Angela as she approached. His eyes looked white and cold. 'Trying to… hold it back…' he croaked. A pained smile appeared on his lips. 'Could do… with a hand…'

Angela nodded immediately and said, 'Come on, Henry!'

Gaskin stepped forward a little uncertainly. 'What can we do?'

'Help them, of course!' Angela grabbed hold of Martha's free hand and held out her other hand towards Gaskin.

He reached out and took it. Her hand felt warm and dry in his. She smiled back at him and said, 'It'll be just like making a wish.'

Duncan joined them, looking up in disgust at the Vurosis. 'That thing bullied its way into my mind, made me kill my best friend!' He grabbed hold of Gaskin's other hand. 'Let's do it!'

The Vurosis suddenly twisted and released a ferocious hiss of annoyance. Green light crackled around the well, discharging into the five people gathered around it in a semi-circle.

The Doctor got to his feet, shakily, but the veins were now settling beneath his skin, and his eyes were shining with renewed determination. 'Keep fighting it,' he said. 'It can't change all of us! That's why it was trying to keep you out!'

The green glow of the telekinetic energy flowed over them, winding around their arms and legs, sparking and crackling but unable to settle. There were too many minds to infiltrate at once.

-i must grow-

'I'm sorry,' the Doctor said. He was looking more like his usual self again, tall, thin, standing up straight as the light flickered over him, his hair moving wildly as the telekinetic force scratched and scraped at his head. He looked directly up at the Vurosis brain, which was now shining with a desperate, blinding green light.

Then the electrical storm of energy surged up and around the well, up the Vurosis itself, concentrating on the brain. Long, jerking fingers of green light stabbed out of the brain, lashing at the humans assembled around it, but without actually connecting. Instead, the wild arcs of light zig-zagged *back towards the creature itself*. Suddenly it was illuminated from within, so brightly that its internal organs were visible through the fibrous outer hide.

The Vurosis thrashed from side to side like a wounded snake. A horrible scream filled the air, tearing through the dome of thorns. Everyone inside and outside covered their ears with their hands, but the noise reverberated inside their heads.

'Look!' shouted the Doctor. Martha couldn't actually hear him over the shrieking, but there was no mistaking what he was pointing to. Cracks were appearing all over the Vurosis, and through the cracks a brilliant, dreadful green light was shining. Its scream reached a terrifying peak and then suddenly the creature blackened, and as it whipped from side to side in its death throes it broke itself apart, crumbling under its own weight. Its skin shredded into nothing, the alien guts inside unravelling and splitting, before finally turning to dust.

The fire spread out through the white weed, searing it away, leaving nothing but ash behind.

'We did it!' Martha yelled, whooping and jumping.

'What did we do?' Gaskin demanded.

'Turned the Vurosis's own power back on itself,' said the Doctor as they watched the weed wither and die. 'It wasn't strong enough to take on all of us. It turned the power right up, but all that happened was that it got caught in its own telekinetic energy field. The transmutation process was accelerated beyond anything it could cope with.'

The last of the weed blackened and faded, revealing the figures of the people that had been caught up in the initial growth. They fell to the ground as soon as the supporting weed disappeared, and Martha instantly ran to help.

The Doctor caught up with her as she knelt by Lucy's prostrate form. Martha looked up at him. 'I don't know if she's alive or not.'

'Let's move her and the others away from here,' he told her. 'It's not over yet.'

There was no time to ask any more questions. The Doctor lifted Lucy onto one shoulder and carried her off the village green, his trainers slipping and sliding in the mud. Several onlookers helped him as he reached the pavement, lifting Lucy down onto a bench. Gaskin and Duncan were carrying another man out between them.

'What's happening now?' Angela asked.

The ground was trembling beneath their feet once more. People were started to panic again, and there was talk of an earthquake.

'The Vurosis had its roots deep underground,' explained the Doctor calmly. 'It's spread out all under the village. It's dying, but the chain reaction is carrying on all the way to its deepest parts.'

People were pulling the thorn brambles away, using gloves or spades or broom handles. The stems simply snapped and broke, crumbling to flakes. Soon the entire dome had caved in as if it were made from straw.

A weak green light shone from the well. It flickered and pulsed as the remainder of the alien being that had been growing for so long beneath the village finally burned away. There was a last, long moan from deep inside the earth and a final, bright flare. Soil and debris spewed out of the well, trailing bits of glowing weed which quickly turned to ash. Slowly the green light died away and all was still and dark.

The village green looked like a battlefield, and there were casualties.

'Stand back, let's have some air here, please...' said Martha, cradling Lucy. The barmaid looked deathly pale and a number of people were crowding around. Martha laid her down and concentrated on clearing the girl's airways, making sure there was nothing left inside her mouth to stop her breathing normally. 'Lucy! Lucy! Can you hear me?'

Lucy's eyes flickered open and she gave a sudden cough, doubling up as if she was choking. Her mouth gagged and she spat out the last bits of weed and soil. The weed crumbled to nothing.

'This one's alive too!' called Duncan, sitting with one of the other men who had been caught in the weeds. He was spluttering too, but holding up a hand to indicate that he would be all right.

The Doctor had wandered back towards the well, which now stood in the middle of a field of churned mud and ash. He picked around in the dirt until he found a small rock, no bigger than a lump of coal. It was grey and weighed next to nothing.

Gaskin joined him. 'What is it?'

'The remains of the Vurosis brain.' The Doctor clenched his fist and the rock crumbled into powder. 'Gone for ever.' He dusted his hands, and the last fragments of the Vurosis blew away on the night air like smoke across a battlefield.

Scattered all around the vicinity of the well were lumps

of soil and rock and general debris thrown up when the Vurosis died.

'This is a right old mess, isn't it?' Gaskin said quietly.

'Oh, the grass will grow back all right,' replied the Doctor. 'And it looks like the well-shaft is still intact.'

'I'm talking about the people who didn't make it. Nigel Carson, Ben Seddon… Old Barney Hackett.'

'Oh, yes, I see.' The Doctor heaved a sigh, as if he had experienced this kind of thing before. 'You have to think of the people who did make it,' he said. 'The people whose lives were saved. And there are an awful lot of those, you know.'

Angela arrived, picking her way carefully through the mud with the help of a borrowed torch. 'Martha's checking over the walking wounded, Doctor,' she said. 'And I've had a call from Sadie Brown. She says she's woken up with a terrible hangover in Henry Gaskin's bed. I think she's more traumatised by that than being turned into an alien monster. Or very nearly, at any rate. She says to thank you and can she turn off that blasted screwdriver thing as it's making her headache worse and driving Jess up the wall. Oh, and she says the manor looks like it's been hit by a bomb.'

'Oh, blast,' said Gaskin. 'I'd forgotten about that!'

'It's going to cost you a fortune to get that repaired,' Angela told him bluntly.

He nodded wryly at the remains of the wishing well. 'And what about this? Bit of a setback for the Creighton Mere Wishing Well Restoration Committee, I should say.'

'Oh, blow,' Angela sighed, looking at the well properly.

'Look at the state of it. Sadie will go bonkers.'

The parapet wall was scorched black and the uprights were no more than pieces of splintered wood. Angela peered down the well-shaft and sighed. 'Not much point in making a wish now, is there?'

'Wait a minute. What's this?' The Doctor was prodding at something in the mud with his toe. It was glinting in the light of Angela's torch near the base of the well.

Gaskin picked it up. 'It's a coin, I think.' He rubbed the mud off with his thumb. 'Good grief. It's gold – look!'

They all peered closely at the coin. 'That's an eighteenth-century gold sovereign,' said the Doctor carefully.

'And there's more, look,' said Angela excitedly, playing the beam of the torch over the ground by their feet. Golden lights reflected all around them.

'Great Scott!' cried Gaskin. 'I don't believe it!'

Martha came running over at the sound of their excited shouts. The Doctor was bending down, brushing soil from a large, leathery object. 'You're not going to believe this,' he said, holding up an old, dirty leather bag. It was mud-stained and rotted, but clearly full and very heavy. As they watched, more gold coins tumbled out of a hole in the ancient stitching.

'It's the treasure!' yelled Martha. 'It's the highwayman's treasure! It really *was* down there all the time!'

'No, it's not the treasure,' said Angela happily. 'It's the Creighton Mere Well and Gaskin Manor Restoration Fund!'

TWENTY-FIVE

The Doctor and Martha stayed on through the night to help collect all the gold sovereigns. Angela used her bush hat to store the coins, and somebody else managed to get their hands on a metal detector to track down the last few pieces lost in the mud. It was an exciting time for everybody, and helped take most people's minds off the terrible events of the evening, at least for a while.

When the police finally arrived, there was little they could do except stare at the muddy village green and scratch their heads. The two constables took statements from a number of people who claimed to be eyewitnesses to an attempted alien invasion of the Earth, starting with Creighton Mere, but in truth the policemen were more confused by the various different accounts of the evening and eventually, finding no actual crime to investigate, they gave up and went away.

And after that, most people did what came naturally:

they went back to the pub. Many of them had left drinks unattended, and found them exactly as they had left them.

Henry Gaskin ordered the largest bottle of fizzy white wine the pub stocked – it would have to do instead of champagne – and paid for drinks all round. Even Jess was treated to a bowl of water by the bar.

Gaskin was elected as Treasurer, a title almost everybody found unaccountably hilarious, and it was unanimously agreed that the proceeds should indeed be used to help rebuild those parts of Gaskin Manor destroyed by the Vurosis, along with a complete re-turfing of the village green, and of course the full and proper restoration of the wishing well.

Sadie Brown decided to put her share towards the setting up of a small tea room adjacent to the village green.

'We'll come back and be your first customers,' Martha assured her happily.

'Make sure you do!' Sadie laughed, making a note of Martha's mobile number and promising to call her as soon as she was ready to open.

Sadie returned the Doctor's sonic screwdriver along with a pot of her Thick-Cut Tawny. She thanked him quietly but honestly for saving her life and kissed him on the cheek. Many people in the pub roared and raised their glasses.

'We really think you ought to take a cut of the loot, you know,' Angela said to the Doctor and Martha. 'After all, if it wasn't for you two…'

'It belongs to the village,' said the Doctor. 'We don't.'

'Take this as a souvenir, then,' Angela said to Martha. She pressed a single gold sovereign into her hand and then closed Martha's fingers over it like a grandmother giving a child pocket money. 'Keep it for luck!'

Martha gaped. 'I can't take this! It's worth a fortune.'

'So are you, dear, so are you.' She looked meaningfully at the Doctor and winked. 'Take care of her, Doctor, won't you?'

He said that he would, and then, with many more hugs and kisses and handshakes, they took their leave. On the way out of the pub, Martha bumped into Duncan again.

'I thought we had a date?' he said, smiling. 'Or are you just teasing me now?'

She could see that he was smiling through some very grim memories. She took him to one side. 'How are you feeling? Really?'

'I can't believe Ben and Nigel are gone.'

'Nigel brought it all on himself, you know. There was nothing you could do.'

'And Ben?'

'Not your doing. None of it was.' Martha held his hand. 'Do you remember much about it?'

'Nothing after that skeleton, no.'

'It's probably best that way.'

'I do remember asking you out, though.' He smiled at her. 'And as much as I know you can't resist me, I'll have to ask you to hold out for a bit longer. I think I'll need a little while to get over all this.'

'Good idea.'

'Angela Hook said I can stay here for as long as I want,

and help out with the well restoration,' Duncan added. 'I think I'd like that.'

Martha kissed him goodbye and went out.

Once again, she found the Doctor waiting for her by the well. He was watching the sunrise.

'I can't keep this,' she said, showing him the gold sovereign Angela had given her.

'Why not?'

'It's too valuable. I mean, it would feel like stealing. I've never owned anything so valuable in all my life.'

The Doctor pulled a face. 'I dunno. There's a planet called Voga that's made from solid gold. They wouldn't be impressed with you there.'

She laughed. 'Maybe not. But all the same…'

He watched her carefully, hands in his pockets, the tails of his long brown coat blowing out behind him. 'So, what are you going to do with it, then?'

'I'm going to make a wish,' she said, holding it out over the well.

'That's a gold sovereign,' he said slowly. 'That's got to be one heck of a wish.'

'We'll make it a double. Have you thought of what you'd wish for yet?'

He shook his head. 'Nah.'

'Go on,' she said, stepping closer. 'There must be something.'

'Nope. Nothing.' His eyes held that faraway look that Martha knew so well. Whatever he was thinking, whatever it was the Doctor secretly wished for, she would never find out. He was, and always would be, a mystery to her.

'Well,' she said eventually, 'looks like I'm going to have to wish for both of us.'

She closed her eyes tight and let go of the coin. Seconds later there was a distinct, echoing plop as it hit water.

She opened her eyes in delight. 'Did you hear that?'

The Doctor was already leaning over the well-shaft, peering down. 'There's water down there! The underground springs must be filling it again. Perhaps the Vurosis had been blocking them for all these years.'

'That's brilliant!'

He grinned at her. 'I love a happy ending, don't you?'

She linked his arm and pulled him away from the well, heading for the TARDIS. 'Always.'

'So what did you wish for?' he asked her.

She smiled. 'Never you mind.'

ACKNOWLEDGEMENTS

Thanks to:

Martine – for patience and help in these busiest of times

Gary Russell and everyone at Cardiff – for letting me play

Justin Richards – for inviting me back on board

Steve Tribe – for editorial advice and suggestions

Moray Laing – for lots of Adventures!

Pete Stam – for being a true and good friend

Dave Cotterill – for buying my books, even though he doesn't watch *Doctor Who*

And David Tennant – *the* Doctor for a new generation

Also available from BBC Books
featuring the Doctor and Martha
as played by David Tennant and Freema Agyeman:

DOCTOR·WHO

Sting of the Zygons
by Stephen Cole
ISBN 978 1 84607 225 3
UK £6.99 US $11.99/$14.99 CDN

The TARDIS lands the Doctor and Martha in the Lake
District in 1909, where a small village has been terrorised
by a giant, scaly monster. The search is on for the elusive
'Beast of Westmorland', and explorers, naturalists and
hunters from across the country are descending on the
fells. King Edward VII himself is on his way to join the
search, with a knighthood for whoever finds the Beast.

But there is a more sinister presence at work in the Lakes
than a mere monster on the rampage, and the Doctor
is soon embroiled in the plans of an old and terrifying
enemy. As the hunters become the hunted, a desperate
battle of wits begins – with the future of the entire world
at stake…

The Last Dodo

by Jacqueline Rayner
ISBN 978 1 84607 224 6
UK £6.99 US $11.99/$14.99 CDN

The Doctor and Martha go in search of a real live dodo,
and are transported by the TARDIS to the mysterious
Museum of the Last Ones. There, in the Earth section,
they discover every extinct creature up to the present day,
all still alive and in suspended animation.

Preservation is the museum's only job – collecting the last
of every endangered species from all over the universe.
But exhibits are going missing…

Can the Doctor solve the mystery before the museum's
curator adds the last of the Time Lords to her collection?

Also available from BBC Books
featuring the Doctor and Martha
as played by David Tennant and Freema Agyeman:

DOCTOR·WHO

Wooden Heart
by Martin Day
ISBN 978 1 84607 226 0
UK £6.99 US $11.99/$14.99 CDN

A vast starship, seemingly deserted and spinning slowly
in the void of deep space. Martha and the Doctor explore
this drifting tomb, and discover that they may not be
alone after all…

Who survived the disaster that overcame the rest of the
crew? What continues to power the vessel? And why has
a stretch of wooded countryside suddenly appeared in the
middle of the craft?

As the Doctor and Martha journey through the forest,
they find a mysterious, fogbound village – a village
traumatised by missing children and prophecies of its
own destruction.

Also available from BBC Books
featuring the Doctor and Martha
as played by David Tennant and Freema Agyeman:

Forever Autumn

by Mark Morris

ISBN 978 1 84607 270 3

UK £6.99 US $11.99/$14.99 CDN

It is almost Halloween in the sleepy New England town of Blackwood Falls. Autumn leaves litter lawns and sidewalks, paper skeletons hang in windows, and carved pumpkins leer from stoops and front porches.

The Doctor and Martha soon discover that something long dormant has awoken in the town, and this will be no ordinary Halloween. What is the secret of the ancient tree and the mysterious book discovered tangled in its roots? What rises from the local churchyard in the dead of night, sealing up the lips of the only witness? And why are the harmless trappings of Halloween suddenly taking on a creepy new life of their own?

As nightmarish creatures prowl the streets, the Doctor and Martha must battle to prevent both the townspeople and themselves from suffering a grisly fate…

Wetworld

by Mark Michalowski

ISBN 978 1 84607 271 0

UK £6.99 US $11.99/$14.99 CDN

When the TARDIS makes a disastrous landing in the
swamps of the planet Sunday, the Doctor has no choice
but to abandon Martha and try to find help. But the
tranquillity of Sunday's swamps is deceptive, and even
the TARDIS can't protect Martha forever.

The human pioneers of Sunday have their own dangers
to face: homeless and alone, they're only just starting to
realise that Sunday's wildlife isn't as harmless as it first
seems. Why are the native otters behaving so strangely,
and what is the creature in the swamps that is so
interested in the humans, and the new arrivals?

The Doctor and Martha must fight to ensure that human
intelligence doesn't become the greatest danger of all.

The Doctor's been everywhere and everywhen in
the whole of the universe and seems to know all the
answers. But ask him what happened to the Starship
Brilliant and he hasn't the first idea. Did it fall into a sun
or black hole? Was it shot down in the first moments
of the galactic war? And what's this about a secret
experimental drive?

The Doctor is skittish. But if Martha is so keen to find
out he'll land the TARDIS on the Brilliant, a few days
before it vanishes. Then they can see for themselves…

Soon the Doctor learns the awful truth. And Martha
learns that you need to be careful what you wish for. She
certainly wasn't hoping for mayhem, death, and badger-
faced space pirates.

Also available from BBC Books
featuring the Doctor and Martha
as played by David Tennant and Freema Agyeman:

Peacemaker

by James Swallow

ISBN 978 1 84607 349 6

UK £6.99 US $11.99/$14.99 CDN

The peace and quiet of a remote homestead in the 1880s American West is shattered by the arrival of two shadowy outriders searching for 'the healer'. When the farmer refuses to help them, they raze the house to the ground using guns that shoot bolts of energy instead of bullets…

In the town of Redwater, the Doctor and Martha learn of a snake-oil salesman whose patent medicines actually cure his patient. But when the Doctor and Martha investigate they discover the truth is stranger, and far more dangerous.

Caught between the law of the gun and the deadly plans of intergalactic mercenaries, the Doctor and Martha are about to discover just how wild the West can become…

DOCTOR·WHO
Starships and Spacestations

by Justin Richards
ISBN 978 1 84607 423 3
£7.99 US $12.99/$15.99 CDN

The Doctor has his TARDIS to get him from place to place and time to time, but the rest of the Universe relies on more conventional transport... From the British Space Programme of the late twentieth century to Earth's Empire in the far future, from the terrifying Dalek Fleet to deadly Cyber Ships, this book documents the many starships and spacestations that the Doctor and his companions have encountered on their travels.

He has been held prisoner in space, escaped from the moon, witnessed the arrival of the Sycorax and the crash landing of a space pig... More than anyone else, the Doctor has seen the development of space travel between countless worlds.

This stunningly illustrated book tells the amazing story of Earth's ventures into space, examines the many alien fleets who have paid Earth a visit, and explores the other starships and spacestations that the Doctor has encountered on his many travels...